STARRING

Minnie Piper

# The Chocolate Cipher

**To the one and only, fabaroonily fantastic Virgil Pomfret, who could out-puzzle anyone! x**
**~ C J**

**To Stan and Becky**
**~ K L**

STRIPES PUBLISHING
An imprint of Magi Publications
1 The Coda Centre, 189 Munster Road, London SW6 6AW

A paperback original
First published in Great Britain in 2009



ISBN: 978-1-84715-083-7



A CIP catalogue record for this book is available from the British Library.

Printed and bound in Belgium.

2 4 6 8 10 9 7 5 3 1

Starring

# Minnie Piper

# The Chocolate Cipher

Caroline Juskus

Illustrated by
Kate Leake

Stripes

# Minnie Piper

It is mind-bogglingly Peculiar that sometimes you think you want things, but when you get them you don't! I haven't a CLUE how it happens but it is make-me-write-things-in-a-spiral-annoying.

Especially as I've wished for oodles of CHOCOLATE... and for the half-term HOLIDAY to not be boring! (yawn) But as Gran always says...

BEWARE WHAT YOU WISH FOR!

A top secret message!

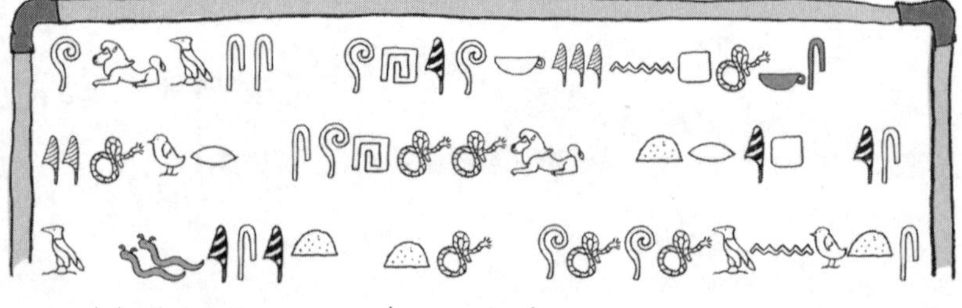

Mr Impey, my whiz teacher, is jumping up and down in his Wednesday-blue tracksuit because he's zingily excited about this top secret message he's just doodled on the board. It's written in artistically ancient letters called *hieroglyphs* and they're almost like a secret code. And, being an undercover puzzler, I'm desperate to try and read what they say because they spell where we're going on our school trip!

That's if Class Chickenpox can finally fill our jar with marbles. We win one every time we're good, and lose one when we're not, and when the Terrible T's, Trevor and Tiffany, are in your class it's a bit like patting your head and rubbing your tummy whilst singing the alphabet backwards in French.

It's taken for ever, but miraculously we've almost done it and we just have two more marbles to collect.  If we can win them by the end of school tomorrow we'll be going on our trip this Friday, which is the last day before half-term!

I'm guessing we'll be visiting the History Museum because it's packed with squillions of Egyptian things and ANCIENT EGYPT is our new project. The only trouble is my best friend, Frankie, is flying off to a wedding in Italy and it'll be a boring trip without her.

"You're so lucky," I whisper to Frankie. "I bet we're going to the History Museum and whilst you're nibbling on pizza in Italy I'll be stuck with Trevor and dinosaurs."

"But I'll be stuck with Nero," laughs Frankie, "and there's NOTHING worse than that!"

And I cannot agree because Frankie's brother is dreamily cool, but I would never tell Frankie so I go back to Mr Impey's message and think the ancient Egyptians were fascinatingly clever because when they stopped ruling, and the Romans took over, nobody else could read their writing. It took hundreds of years and millions of brain cells to finally decipher…

A B C D E

F G H I J

K L M N O

P Q R S T

U V W X Y

Z

So far I have decoded CLASS CHICKENPOX YOUR SCHOOL TRIP IS A VISIT TO … and I'm sure it's going to be THE HISTORY MUSEUM so I go to the letter T, but most peculiarly I'm not right.

"That's odd," I whisper to Frankie. "I don't think it's the History Museum after all. It's somewhere beginning with C."

"Maybe it's Cleopatra's Museum?"

"I've never heard of that," I tell her.

"Nor me!" she giggles. "But maybe it's in another town and you have to go by bus."

And she could be right because Cleopatra is

definitely something to do with Egypt so I look up the next letter in the secret message, but it's not L, it's O. Followed by C, another O and A!

"It spells COCOA!" gasps Frankie, deciphering with me. "Quick, Minnie, it might say..."

"It can't!" I squeal!

But just in case I frantically check the remaining letters and they all appear as if by magic. I wave my arms and bounce up and down and Trevor hollers, "Minnie Piper's got ants in 'er pants!"

"Haven't!" I tell him. "I've cracked the secret message!"

"Fantastic!" grins Mr Impey. "Come and write it on the board please, Minnie."

Trevor pings me with an elastic band, but I'm so excited that I jump up and completely ignore him and sweetly scribble...

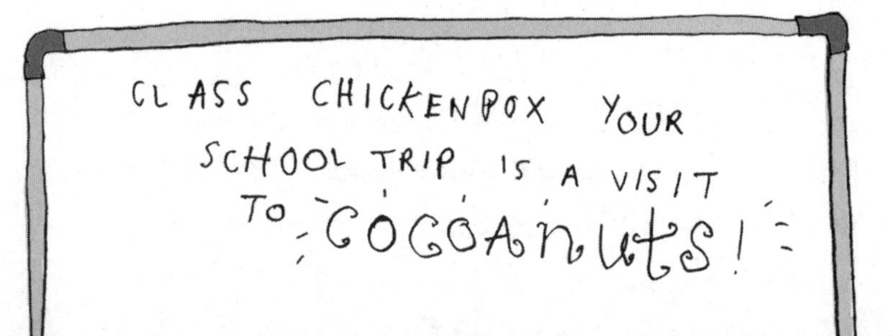

"Cocoanuts is nuts about cocoa!" shouts Frankie.

And we've all heard the advert a zillion times, and I've always wanted to go for a visit and can barely believe that in two days' time I'll be nibbling my way round their chocolate factory!

"THE Cocoanuts?!" ask Delilah and Tallulah. And they ask at exactly identical times because they're exactly identical look-alike twins.

"THE Cocoanuts," agrees Mr Impey. "But first you must win one more marble. Minnie's just won one for cracking the message, but you still need another to fill your jar. And of course, you mustn't lose any either."

Everybody stares at Trevor, who's the naughtiest boy on the whole of the planet.

"Don't worry," says Mr Impey. "I'm sure Trevor will behave for the next two days. And to start him off, he can hand out these letters for your parents' permission that I'll need back tomorrow."

Trevor takes them and, on his politest behaviour, passes them round.

"I don't need one!" grumbles Frankie sulkily. "I won't be here on Friday."

"All the more chocolates for us then!" snorts Trevor, whose manners have already slipped to his socks.

I glare at him, but I can't shout back as I don't want to lose us a marble. So I cross my fingers and mumble a wish that he loses his voice before he loses us our trip. And irritatingly Tiffany hears me and crosses her fingers, too, and I'm just scribbling copycat when the bell goes and it's time to go home.

## WEDNESDAY NIGHT

### I love ice cream

Living in a flat in Arthurs Way is non-stop noisy. There are cats wailing in our shared concrete garden and boys kicking cans instead of footballs and Spike, my baby brother, howling because he's trying to cut a new tooth. He's hollered ever since I've been back from school, and this is annoying as it's Frankie's birthday this Monday and I'm trying to design her a birthday card, but it's impossible to think of what to doodle when your brother sounds like a fire alarm. And it's especially irritating as I'm trying to make the card extra special because I won't see her for four whole days. And I probably won't see her much in the holiday either, because Mum is painting a mural in a flower shop, which means I have to stay with Gran.

"Could Frankie come to Gran's, too?" I ask Mum.

"Maybe," she replies. "But don't forget Spike will be there, and Gran might find it too much."

I look at Spike who is now screeching on top of Dad's head. Dad's zooming round the room like a motorbike and I'm not sure if he thinks Spike will like this or if he's trying to drown him out. But either way, I remember back to this afternoon and Frankie moaning about Nero. If she thinks being stuck with HER brother is bad, then how would she cope with mine? Maybe I shouldn't invite her over, but if I don't the holiday's going to be boring. It's so hard to decide with all the noise and it gets even noisier when the phone rings, but it's Frankie trying to speak to me before she goes to Italy!

"What's that racket, Minnie?" she cringes. "Are you watching a scary film?"

"It's Spike screaming," I tell her. "And Dad being a motorbike. You'll have to talk loudly, I can barely hear you."

"I was thinking about the holiday," she shouts.

"You're so lucky!" I sigh. "I wish I was going to Italy."

"And miss out on the trip to Cocoanuts! I wish I could stay behind with you. But I wasn't thinking about that holiday, I was thinking about half-term."

"And me," I tell her. "I was thinking you could come to Gran's, but Spike will be there and he'll be really noisy."

"OR..." hollers Frankie, "you could come to MY place! Mum has to stay in Italy and Dad's worrying how he'll manage at the Deli. He's asked me to help him make the pizzas and I wondered if you'd like to help him too?"

"Of course I would!" I yell excitedly. "I absolutely love pizzas!" Frankie's dad owns Minelli's Deli and it's the yummiest place in the whole of Hill Tops.

"Fabaroony!" shouts Frankie. "We can serve ice creams too, and help in the shop. The only trouble is that Nero will be there and he's bringing a friend and they're bound to be smelly."

"Not as smelly as Spike!" I grin. "Or as noisy. And I love ice cream!"

"That's true," laughs Frankie. "I'll see

you on Monday, then. Byeeee, Minnie!"

"Bye, Frankie. Have fun in Italy."

"I will." And she puts down the phone and I can't help smiling because it might just be the best half-term ever!

## THURSDAY AT SCHOOL

### Hot ~~chocolate~~ TREVOR

This morning over breakfast, whilst Mum was signing the permission-to-go-to-Cocoanuts letter, I made another wish – a wish that today would zoom flea-hoppingly fast so that I wouldn't have time to miss Frankie. And Trevor wouldn't have time to cause any trouble and so far it seems to be working. This morning zipped by and we had to doodle Egyptianish things and I drew the Sphinx, a famous statue, which reminds me a bit of Wanda Wellingtons. Wanda is my loopy fluffy dog and when she's waiting to be fed she sits totally still in front of her bowl with her head up and her front paws facing inwards, exactly like the Sphinx. She's the best dog ever and is probably cleverer than Trevor. Though Trevor's so desperate to go to Cocoanuts that he actually passed his spelling test this morning, which means we've finally won our last marble!

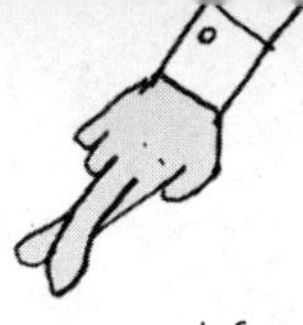

Now we just need to stay good for the rest of the day and I'm crossing my fingers extra tightly and Mr Impey is bouncing up and down in his cherry-red tracksuit beaming, "Only 35 minutes to the end-of-school bell! Stay good, Chickenpoxers, and keep your marbles because I've a very special announcement to make. Cocoanuts have been studying Egypt, too, and it's inspired them to invent a new chocolate. It looks like a pyramid and we're going to be the first to try it!"

Class Chickenpox hums like a beehive. Kevin wants to know what flavour it will be and Jasen wants to know how big it will be, only his throat is sore and it hurts him to speak and Abhi has to ask it for him.

Mr Impey is brain-spinningly clever and always knows the answers to everything, but this time he says, "I haven't a clue, but it will probably be bite-size and chocolaty."

"Even I knew that," grumbles Trevor.

But Mr Impey ignores him and says, "That's not all. Cocoanuts are holding a Chocolate Pyramid Competition, and whoever gets the right answer wins a WHOLE YEAR'S SUPPLY!

We hum even louder and I glance at Trevor, who's sweet mad, and hope this might keep him on his best behaviour. His cheeks are glowing, so it looks as though he's tickled pink.

Next we learn about the competition and how we'll need to solve a keyword Cipher. It sounds a bit tricky, but Mr Impey explains that Ciphers are just a type of puzzle. And as puzzles are my absolute speciality I watch excitedly as he scribbles RENRNJPUM on the board.

"Is that it?" asks Abhi.

"It's a secret message," says Mr Impey. "A secret message written with a keyword Cipher." And in a wonky-but-should-be-straight line beneath it, he prints the alphabet from A to Z and says, "To read my secret message you need to know the keyword. The keyword is the secret part of a Cipher and you must keep it hidden from anyone that you don't want to read your message."

My eyes light up because secret messages are super-sleuth cool!

"A keyword can be any word the code inventor chooses," explains Mr Impey, "but today, because we're learning about them in history, and hoping to eat them at Cocoanuts tomorrow, the keyword is PYRAMID." And he writes it beneath the first seven letters of the alphabet, lining it up painstakingly neatly. "And now for the tricky part...!"

secret message = RENRNJPUM

alphabet = A B C D E F G
P Y R A M I D

Trevor sighs and looks redder than ever as Mr Impey continues with, "To finish the Cipher we write the rest of the alphabet in its correct order, following on from the last letter of the keyword. In this case the last letter of PYRAMID is D, so the next letter will be E, then F, and we continue like this, lining up the letters beneath our original alphabet, but missing out those we have in our keyword." And he keeps scribbling till it looks like this…

secret message = RENRNJPUM

alphabet = A B C D E F G H I J K L M N O P Q R S T U V W X Y Z
cipher = P Y R A M I D E F G H J K L N O Q S T U V W X Z B C

"To read the secret message," he says, "you must find each of its letters in the Cipher line. Then look for the letters above them. For example, the last letter in the message is M. Find M in the Cipher and above it is E. This means the last letter of the message is E. Now you need to finish the rest."

And I cannot believe it is that simple and maybe, just maybe, I might win the competition! I begin to scribble and I've just got the first letter, C, when I'm

interrupted by a familiar voice. It's my cling-on cousin, Dot, and her teacher, Mrs Elliott, and I've no idea what they're doing here, but it's typical of Dot to interrupt my fun. And I'm not the only one being distracted. Tiffany Me-Me has to step outside. Mr Impey goes with her and two minutes later they both return with Tiffany looking very upset. She opens her bag and hands Mr Impey a book and Dot beams and nods her head and waves at me grinning, "*Bonjour*, Minnie!"

Cringingly I wave back, but thankfully no one sees me because everybody is staring at Tiff. And I know exactly what book she's handed over – Dot's French dictionary. Dot's been practising how to speak French because she's going to France on Saturday to stay with her mum. Mrs Elliott ushers her out of the classroom and Mr Impey looks very stern and says, "What do you have to say, Tiffany?"

"Sorry," says Tiff, staring at her boots. And they're such nice boots, with pointy toes and high heels, that they almost distract me from what's coming next.

"And why are you sorry?" asks Mr Impey.

"Because I took Dot's book," says Tiff.

"AND?"

"I've lost a marble from our marble jar."

Class Chickenpox gasps.

"Trust YOU!" croaks Trevor.

"Can't she just not come to Cocoanuts?" asks Abhi.

"Sorry," says Mr Impey, "but it's a class effort. Now please get back to work on the Cipher." And he sits at his desk and looks at the pictures we drew this morning.

But none of us can think about the Cipher. We've got less than five minutes to win another marble or we're NOT going to Cocoanuts! Everybody glowers at Tiff and we're all so cross that we secretly hope that Trevor will give her her just desserts and tie her plait to the back of her chair. But Trevor doesn't move. His cheeks are now burning and he's slumped across his desk. And then I cannot believe it, but Tiffany passes me a note saying… *'Sorry Minnie. I didn't really take your cousin's book.'*

How can she say this when we've just seen the evidence? Tiffany always wants what isn't hers and I know she is fibbing because Dot takes her dictionary everywhere and this afternoon she didn't have it and Tiffany Me-Me did. I turn the note over and scribble, *'PANTS ON FIRE!'* and send it back.

Mr Impey coughs loudly, which usually means that someone's in trouble, and I'm pretty sure that someone is me and he's seen me passing the note. But peculiarly it isn't and he says, "Trevor Bottomley, can you come here, please?" He must think Trevor's fallen asleep which means we've probably lost another marble.

Abhi prods Trevor and Trevor croaks, "Leave it out, Talwar, I 'eard." And he gets up and there are crease marks on his red face where it's been pressed against his sleeve.

"Are you all right?" asks Mr Impey. "You look a bit hot."

"Never felt better," snorts Trevor. But I know he is fibbing because he's totally crimson and almost the colour of Mr Impey's tracksuit.

"Perhaps you could explain this drawing then?" asks Mr Impey, holding up a picture that's a cross between our marble jar and a very vicious eagle. By its side is a string of sausages sitting in a puddle of blood and, typically of Trevor, it's realistically brilliant, but stomach-churningly horrid. Beneath it, in some sort of secret code, he has printed QEBEHSENUEF. Trust Trevor to draw this. I should have known he wasn't being good, even though he was pretending he was.

"It's a canopic jar," he croaks. "It's wot ancient Egyptians put dead people's intestines in. And this is Qebehsenuef, a falcon 'oo guards them."

Mr Impey bobs up and down like a giddy red parrot and to our surprise he isn't cross. "Brilliant!" he exclaims. "In fact it's so good I'm going to award you ... a marble!"

Trevor looks stunned, but not as stunned as the rest of us. "Does that mean...?" shouts Kevin Little.

"Yes!" grins Mr Impey. "Thanks to Trevor you WILL be going to Cocoanuts!"

And we can barely believe it, and there are only two minutes until the end-of-school bell. I make a wish that time will pass quickly and try to beat the clock by finishing the Cipher. And as the bell rings I doodle

RENRNJPUM = CHOCOLATE!

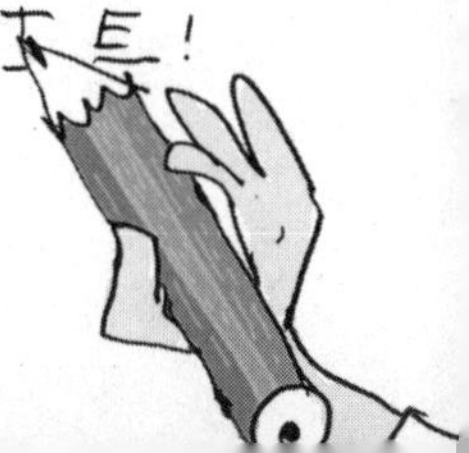

## THURSDAY EVENING

### Hot Trevor and hot chocolate

After school I have to babysit Dot, and she's get-on-your-nerves *très* annoying because she won't stop speaking in French. I'm trying to watch the TV, but Dot is stroking Wanda cooing, "*Bonjour, Wanda. Je m'appelle Dot.*" And Wanda is the cleverest dog on the planet and already knows she is called Dot, but before I can knowingly point this out, Spike wakes up and won't stop screaming. And I am just beginning to wonder which is worse, Dot speaking French or Spike hollering, when Wanda starts barking because she's seen a cat on the telly. And the flat is so noisy that I have to escape!

"I think Wanda needs a walk," I tell Mum. "I could take her to the park if you like, then Dad won't have to do it when he comes back from work."

"Good idea," says Mum.

"Can I come?" asks Dot.

"*Non!*" I tell her.

But Mum says, "Of course you can, Dot. Minnie can drop you home when you've finished."

Crossly I grab Wanda's lead and head for the door and as we set off through Arthurs Way, Dot sings "Frère Jacques". My luck doesn't improve when we get to the park because Trevor is sitting on a swing with his football, and Tyson, Tiffany's humungous dog, is watching her brothers, Otis and Presley, skateboard on a ramp. Otis and Presley are a little bit scary and Tyson is hugely, EXTREMELY scary. He's bigger than me and boisterously bouncy and always wants to chase Wanda.

"I don't like Presley and Otis," sniffs Dot. "They took my book."

"THEY took your book? I thought it was Tiffany?"

"Tiffany took it off Otis," says Dot, "to stop him getting into trouble."

"Dot," I sigh, "now Tiffany's in trouble. Did you tell Mrs Elliot this?"

"I told her Tiffany took my book."

"But she was probably going to give it back to you."

"The bell went for the end of playtime and I didn't want to do waiting," sniffs Dot.

"But why did Otis take your book?"

"Because I did speaking to him in French and he didn't like it and asked me to stop."

"And did you stop?"

"*Non,*" sniffs Dot.

"But if boys like that ask you to stop speaking in French, then you stop speaking in French! They're nasty bullies and they'll pick on you."

"But I like speaking in French," says Dot.

"I know you do, but sometimes you must learn when to stop."

Dot's bottom lip trembles. "I need to be able to talk to Mum."

"But your mum still speaks English, Dot! She hasn't forgotten it because she's living in France."

"Are you sure?" she asks. "Mum always says *Bonjour* on the phone."

And she looks so worried that I'm afraid she's about to burst into tears. She hasn't seen her mum for weeks and she's really missing her, so to cheer her up I let her take hold of Wanda's lead.

Dot smiles, but suddenly Presley has noticed her and hollers, "Oy, you, French girl! I 'ear you got my sister into trouble!"

"Ignore him," I whisper to Dot. "We're going to turn around and head back home and I don't want you to say a word to them ... in French or English. D'you understand?"

"*Oui,*" sniffs Dot.

But Presley and Otis have other plans, and before we have gone ten steps they are skateboarding our way with Tyson charging straight for Wanda! Dot runs away speedily fast, which is surprising for a cling-on with such short legs. But Tyson chases anything that moves and Dot, who is still holding Wanda's lead, is definitely moving!

"Stop him!" I order, but Otis and Presley just laugh and before I can act Tyson has bounced upon poor Dot and sent her flying. She and Wanda are both shaking and just when things can't get any worse Trevor arrives to join in the fight. I might have known he

was Otis's friend, and he dribbles his football about my feet as if trying to trip me up. He's red and sweaty and his breath stinks of cabbage and socks as he looks at me threateningly and mouths, "Get lost, Piper. D'you understand? When I say go, you go!"

"Get lost, yourself, Trevor!" I tell him. "You can't bully me."

But he hoarsely croaks, "GO!" and kicks his ball so hard it's as if he's in the World Cup and the future of his team depends upon him. I've never seen a ball kicked quite that far and Tyson immediately chases after it and Trevor wheezes,

"Get out of 'ere Piper!"

At last I see what Trevor is doing! He isn't bullying me at all, he's saving me by distracting Tyson!

"Thanks," I whisper, but Trevor has gone, pretending as if nothing ever happened. But Otis has seen him and is calling him names and whilst he and Presley start picking on Trevor, I gather up Dot and Wanda and quickly head for Arthurs Way.

We're all OK, but Dot's scraped her knee and Uncle Jeff sticks a plaster on it and makes us mugs of hot chocolate. It's sugarly sweet and when Dot says it's *très bon* for once I have to agree.

When I get home my tea is on the swinging table and it's broccoli and noodles and it's definitely NOT *très bon*. Mum's got a new yoga teacher and her name is Mina and she's totally healthy and Mum is trying to be like her. We've always had to eat wholefoods, but now Mum's even stricter and sugar is banned except on Saturdays. From Sunday to Friday there are no biscuits, no cakes, no ice creams, and most annoyingly, NO CHOCOLATE.

But not tomorrow. Tomorrow I'm going to Cocoanuts!

# FRIDAY DAY

## Cocoanuts

I am sitting next to Abhi on the coach and Mr Impey has just announced that we're ten minutes away from Cocoanuts! Abhi is my partner for the day, which isn't as good as Frankie Minelli, but is not as bad as Trevor or Tiff. Tiff is partners with Brainiac Jenny (because Jenny is nice and the only person not to protest) and Jasen and Trevor are both off sick. I can't help feeling sorry for them, especially Trevor as he did win us the last marble. And saved me in the park yesterday, even though he wasn't well.

Abhi saw Mrs Bottomley this morning, and apparently Trevor has the mumps which is why he was sweaty and red in the face. But the worst of it is it's MY fault. I made a wish for him to lose his voice and now he has and his neck has swollen so he looks like a hippo and his throat is so sore he can barely swallow his own earwax let alone delicious chocolate.

But I tuck this to the back of my mind because we have just got to Cocoanuts! Another two schools are visiting as well and we all squash into the entrance hall that looks more like a jungle! Towering over us are plastic palm trees, and hanging beneath their shiny green leaves are bunches of chocolate brown coconuts! Clinging to the trunks are clockwork hairy monkeys and when you wind their tails they scamper up the trees singing, "Cocoanuts is nuts about cocoa!"

Tiffany Me-Me pushes forward and says, "Me, me, me, I want to wind up the tail!" but luckily a man in a hairnet blows a whistle and we have to pay attention and form a group.

I've never seen a man in a hairnet before but Abhi says it is probably, definitely to stop his hair from falling in the chocolate.

It's hard to take the man seriously, especially when he says his name is Brian Willy Wonka Wilson. He's in a white coat and wellingtons and says, "Welcome to Cocoanuts! Does anybody here like chocolate?"

A hundred arms wave in the air and Brian says, "Then follow me!"

And we can barely wait, and we push our way into the factory that is packed with machines that make Cocoanuts chocolate! It smells delicious and Brian explains it's where milk and sugar get mixed with cocoa, and numerous top secret ingredients.

"What top secret ingredients?" asks Abhi.

Abhi's a boffin and always wants to know these things, but because they're secret Brian won't tell him. At least I think he won't. It's hard to hear because the machines are so noisy and most of the workers have little foam sausages plugged in their ears to help deaden the sound.

At the end of each machine is a conveyor belt and it's a bit like being in a supermarket but, instead of carrying carrots to a till, the belts carry chocolates. And WE get to try them! There are zillions of flavours and I gobble down zingy chilli, fruity raspberry, and would-like-it-as-toothpaste breath-fresh peppermint. A lady with a badge saying *Cleopatra CHOCOLATE TESTER* asks me which I like best, but my taste buds are jiggling on the tip of my tongue and I truthfully tell her that I can't decide.

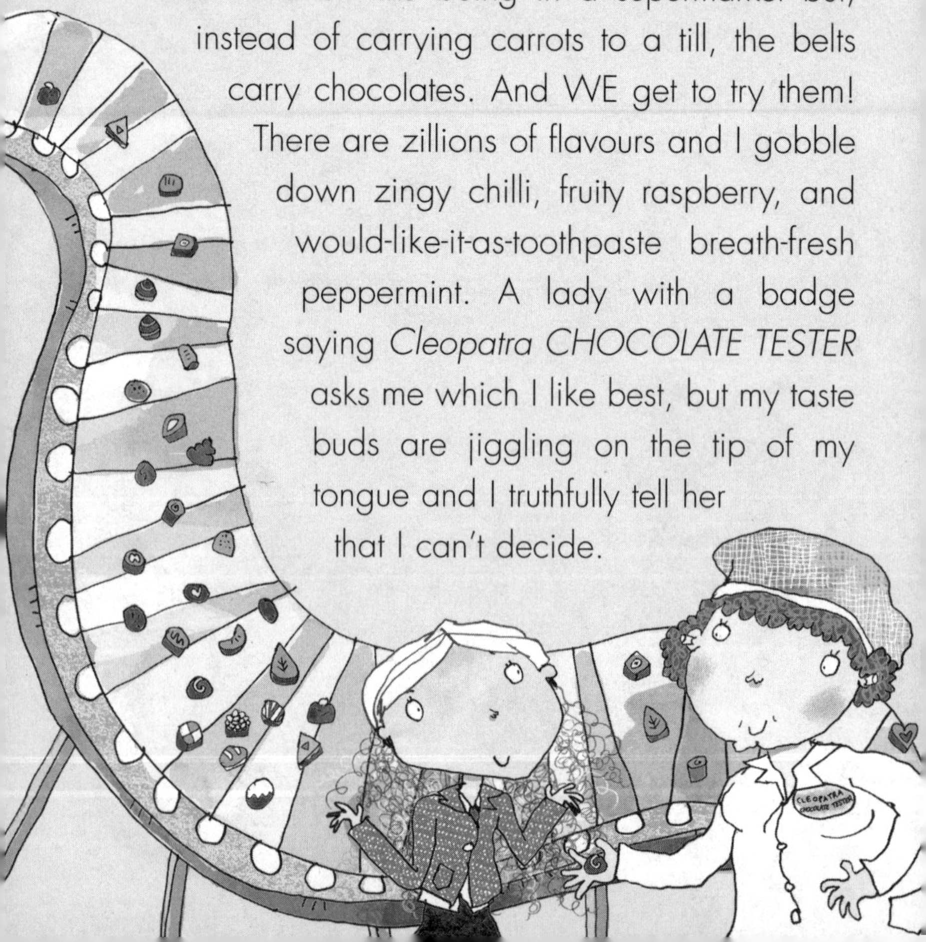

"Sorry," she smiles, "I didn't hear you. Oh, I've forgotten to take my earplugs out!"

And she removes her foam sausages as I bellow, "I can't decide which I like the best!"

"Goodness!" beams the lady, who can now hear me loud and clear. "Then I'd better give you a few more."

And taste-tinglingly brilliantly she gives me another six chocolates to help me make up my mind! And I've never known what I want to be when I grow up, but now I've decided! I'm going to be a chocolate tester! Someone has to do it and it might as well be me! And spicy chocolate orange is definitely my favourite and Cleopatra nods and ticks a box.

Next we watch wrappers being printed and slipped over bars of chocolate. And then Brian moves us on and we stare goggle-eyed as boxes are stuffed with our favourite sweets, all twisted in brightly-coloured cellophane and tied shut with a ribbon. But too soon it's time for lunch, though I'm so full from testing chocolate that I can barely nibble a thing.

Mr Impey's in his Friday-black tracksuit and looks like a sandwich-gobbling stick of liquorice with a mad mop of hair. He's talking to Brian Willy Wonka Wilson and Brian winks and hands him a gold envelope that Mr Impey stashes in his bag.

"What d'you think that was?" whispers Abhi.

"A hairnet!" I giggle. "Brian probably thinks Mr Impey needs one."

And then Brian blows his whistle and asks if we're ready for more of the tour. Everyone nods and he grins. "I hope you'll find this next room very exciting. No one but the staff of Cocoanuts have been in, and no one but them has tried our new chocolate. You'll be the first, so fingers crossed that you're going to like it."

And I'm so glad I didn't eat much lunch because he adds, "You may all try as many as you like, but in return could you please complete a questionnaire. Now, if everyone's ready, follow me!" And he takes off his hairnet and his hair's stuck flattish to his head and we all follow hot on his heels as if we are in a Chocolate trance.

Everyone pushes in a desperate attempt to be the first, but if the entrance hall was like a jungle, this room is like ANCIENT EGYPT. The floor is covered in golden sand and the walls are made out of fake stone, carved and chiselled with *hieroglyphics*, or painted with pictures of mummies and pharaohs! And none of the staff are wearing hairnets, but are wrapped in togas, even Brian, who must've been hiding his under his coat! The ladies have black painted around their eyes, and in their hands are platters of jewels, which on closer inspection are gold chocolates!

"They must be the pyramids!" whispers Abhi.

And as if Brian has supersonic hearing, he blows his whistle and assembles us in front of a large banner of glitzy gold paper saying:

Cocoanuts

proudly present

THE *Chocolate* GOLD PYRAMID!

And he cuts a string and the paper drops to reveal a sparkling gold pyramid. And it's even taller than Brian and is actually a pyramid made out of Chocolate Gold Pyramids!

Da-daaah!

"Da-daaah!" sings Brian, as we each get handed three chocolates. They look so nice that it's almost a shame to have to peel one, but I tear off the foil and bite the top and gooey caramel spills down my chin. And I don't care because it's so delicious!

"Let's guess what the secret ingredients are," whispers Abhi.

"Toffee," I tell him.

"And vanilla," nods Abhi.

And we fill out the questionnaires and we're supposed to award them marks out of ten, but me and Abhi give them eleven, though we each nibble another three to make trebly sure that we're telling the truth!

"This has been the best school day ever," says Abhi.

"Perhaps we could get ourselves locked in!" I suggest.

And we're about to plan where we might hide when Brian blows his whistle for the very last time. He wishes us a safe journey home, and hopes we had a fun day and that we'll tell everyone how yummy his chocolates are. And we all nod as

Cleopatra whispers something in his ear.

"Oh, yes!" grins Brian. "I almost forgot! To help celebrate our new chocolate you're all going to get a goody bag of Pyramids and a chance to win a year's supply! Your teachers have the details and the goody bags!"

And just like Brian, I'd completely forgotten about the competition! How scrummy is that?! A dreamily delicious Chocolate Gold Pyramid could drop through my letterbox and on to my tongue every day for a whole year! And it means leaving Cocoanuts is not so sad because I've got something tasty to look forward to. And a goody bag!

On the coach back to school Mr Impey opens Brian's envelope and I nudge Abhi and whisper, "Here comes the hairnet." But Abhi's feeling queasy because the vibrations of the coach are stirring up all the chocolate in his tummy. Plus it's not a hairnet! It's a stack of gold paper.

"This," says Mr Impey, "is Cleopatra's Chocolate Competition! I'll put one into each of your goody bags."

And I can hardly wait and I pay no attention to what he says next as it contains the words half-term and homework.

And then the coach pulls up outside of school and Mr Impey hands me a gold bag bursting with chocolates and a sheet of gold paper headed:

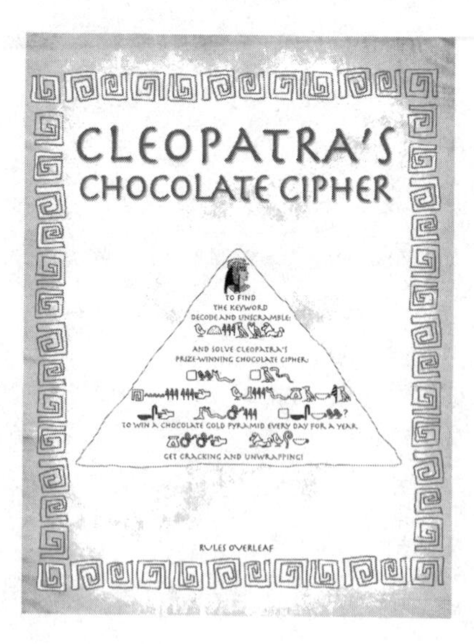

# FRIDAY NIGHT

## Chocolates and ciphers

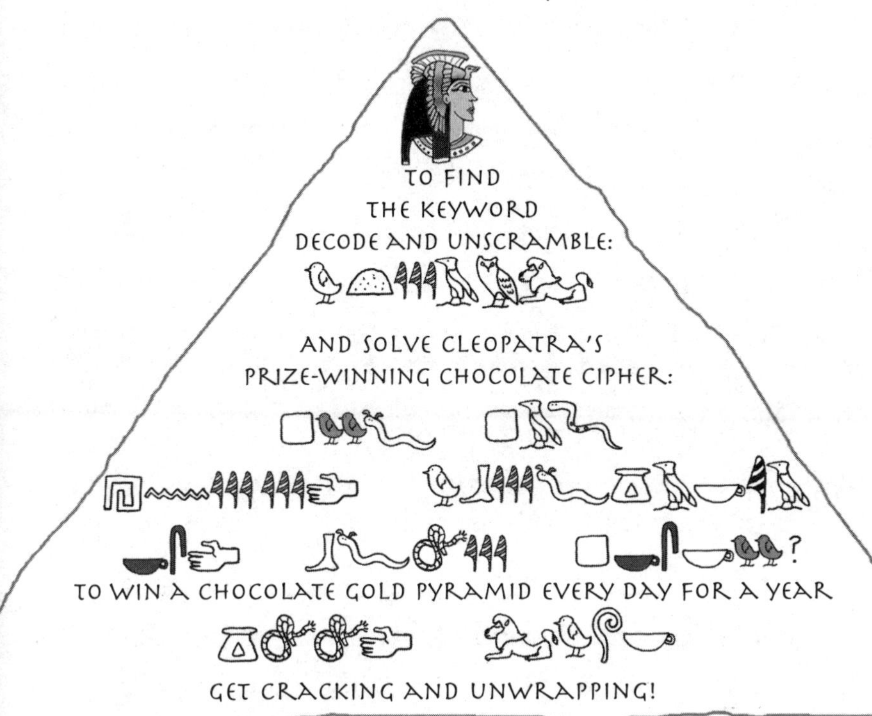


It looks hieroglyphically brilliant and I'm in bed nibbling a Chocolate Gold Pyramid puzzling how to solve it! There were twenty of them in my goody bag, but the problem is that eating chocolate in bed is strictly banned and the Pyramid cracked open like a caramel volcano and has spilt down my pyjamas.

I'm just panicking how I'll explain this to Mum when, bad-timing annoyingly, she shouts, "Have you turned your light out, Minnie?"

"Not yet," I tell her. "I've got something important to do."

"Nothing's so important that it can't wait until morning," she replies.

And this is totally untrue as the Chocolate Cipher can't wait another minute, let alone twelve hours. But I can't tell Mum this as she doesn't see the urgency in solving secret messages, even when they come with a mouth-watering prize.

So I pull my duvet up to my chin and when the chocolate stain on my PJs is hidden I try my luck with, "Actually it can't wait. I've got a might-melt-might-get-nibbled-by-Wanda kind of present for you and Dad."

"Why didn't you say so?" grins Dad, poking his head around my bedroom door.

Then he sits on my bed and swings his holey-socked feet off the floor and Mum comes in with Spike in her arms, who's wailing like a cat with a mousetrap on its tail. I rummage in my goody bag and Dad's eyes light up when I give him a Chocolate Gold Pyramid. I explain about the competition and

Mum says it sounds deliciously educational and as it's almost Saturday perhaps she can bend the rules a little and we can all eat a Pyramid now! And she doesn't know I've had seven today! Or that this will be my SECOND in ten minutes!

"I like this competition!" says Dad.

"Me too!" I smile.

But Spike doesn't. He's still howling and Mum says, "I think you'd better do the Cipher in the morning, Minnie."

"Can I just have five more minutes?" I ask.

"Two," says Mum, "and I'm already counting."

Then she and Dad disappear and I stare quickly at...

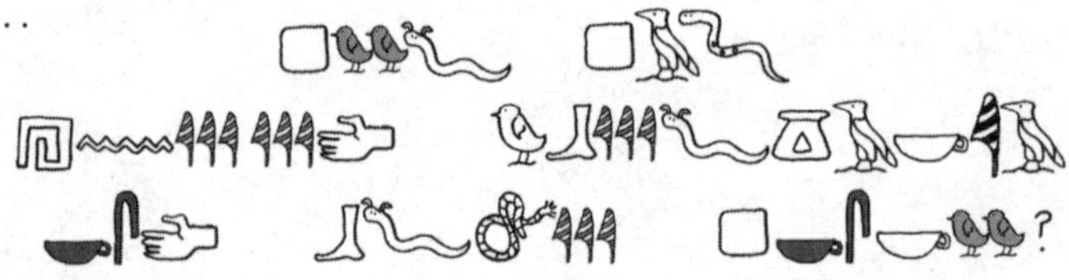

I don't have time to look for my sheet of hieroglyphics and the only ones I can remember are M, A, P for Minnie Apple Piper. M is an owl , A is a vulture and P is a square thing that Mr Impey said is a stool, and there are three stools and three vultures in the Chocolate Cipher! This means I know it contains P P A A A P! But there's not a wise old owl in sight, so that means no M's, and I'm speedily progressing as fast as an ancient Egyptian snail.

Although Spike's in another room I can still hear him screaming and it's deafeningly hard to think. I look at the keyword, , and the fourth hieroglyph is another vulture and finally I've found an M! The keyword says _ _ _ A M _!

And then I switch my attention to the last line but annoyingly it doesn't contain any owls, vultures or stools. But my minutes are up and Dad comes back to turn out my light.

As he does he giggles, "What did the P say to the O, when O ate all the chocolates?"

"I don't know," I sigh.

"That's not fair, O! Pharaoh, get it? P...H...A...R...A...O...H! Ancient king of Egypt."

"That's AWFUL!" I tell him.

"Not as awful as Spike's wailing!" groans Dad.

And he leaves with both his thumbs in his ears and Wanda sneaks in and together we hide under the covers to try and drown out the row. It's hard to see so I flick on my alien pen and the alien's head lights up and in an eerie green glow I sneak another peak at the Chocolate Cipher. But Wanda's not interested in cracking Ciphers, she's ready to sleep. And yawningly annoyingly so am I. I tell her about Cocoanuts and their different types of chocolate before we sweetly fall into our best dream ever.

# SATURDAY DAY

## Love Hearts and Parma Violets

Today's going to be my lucky day because Uncle Jeff's taking Dot to France, which means there'll be a sea between us and Dot is not a good swimmer.

It's also my allowed-to-nibble-sugar day and me and Dad are in a spangly new sweet shop called Psychodelicious! Its walls are painted bubblegum pink and it has a pathway winding through it that looks as though someone has spilled a lorry-load of Smarties. Dad buys himself a candyfloss and white chocolate buttons for Spike and, because it sounds exotic, and Mina might approve, a box of Turkish Delight for Mum. He waits outside while I try to decide what to get for me, but as usual I can't make up my mind. Then a wish-I-could-be-like-her sort of girl smiles at me and says hello and she's everything that I'm not, totally confident and cool. She just goes ahead and picks three tubes of LOVE HEARTS and two tubes of PARMA VIOLETS. No dithering or wondering what would be the best, she just seems to know.

I wish I could make decisions like that and I can't stop looking at her short black hair, pointy boots and hat pulled over one of her eyes. In an instant I want to look like her too and when she has gone I grab three tubes of LOVE HEARTS and two tubes of PARMA VIOLETS and strut off to pay.

Dad has a sugary candyfloss moustache that wiggles as he says, "Next stop the motorbike shop! We need to get you a crash helmet, Minnie!"

"A crash helmet?!" I exclaim. "Am I going to ride on your bike?"

"I hope so!" laughs Dad. "You'll sit on the back. It's called riding pillion."

And I'm lost for words as I never knew I'd be doing this! And he marches off because he's so excited that his bike is nearly finished. He's been mending it for ages as it's practically as ancient as an Egyptian pyramid, but at last it's almost back together and we head for a shop called DAVE'S BIKES. It is nothing at all like Psychodelicious but Dave is nice and tries not to get annoyed when my mad poodle hair gets in the way of trying on helmets. Eventually I find one that fits and it's white with purple flames on the side and Dad says it's perfect and I have to agree, and as we head home we can't stop smiling.

I've never been on a motorbike before and I can't quite decide if it'll be scarily brilliant or scarily horrid. But what IS definitely scarily horrid is the spinach smoothie Mum serves for lunch. Dad says it looks like liquidized caterpillars, but Mum says it is bursting with healthfulness and is her yoga teacher's favourite. I close my eyes, so as not to see it, and it spills down my hoody leaving zingy green stains. At least this means there is less to swallow and accidentally on purpose I drop half a slice of tofu prune cake and Wanda devours it as if it was a tub of toffee ice cream. Ten minutes later I'm in my room dreaming about Minelli's Deli pizza instead of Mum's awful wholefoods.

I pop a PARMA VIOLET on my tongue and it scentily takes the spinach taste away. But now it feels like I've swallowed Gran's perfume. I decide it's best to stick to LOVE HEARTS and unravel the tube and the one on the top says BE MINE. I instantly obey and place it in my mouth and it tastes so delicious that I stop thinking about peculiar flavours and concentrate on hieroglyphics.

hieroglyphics are mind-bogglingly more interesting than our own alphabet and I decide I'll use them to write Frankie a special message. For her birthday I'm going to give her ten Pyramids from my goody bag and a hieroglyphic message would be perfect to go with them. The only trouble is that the hieroglyphs for F, J and V are scaly snakes and anything scaly makes me shudder. Even Trevor doesn't send me into such a hard-to-breathe panic and my legs are just starting to turn to jelly when the phone rings and it's Gran.

"Hi, Gran."

"Hello, Minnie. I hear you're entering a chocolate competition. Your dad seems very excited."

"That's because you get to win a year's supply of Chocolate Gold Pyramids!" I tell her. And I explain about the Chocolate Cipher and how it's written in hieroglyphics, but that three hieroglyphs are scaly snakes and I don't like looking at them. "Plus right now I'm trying to write Frankie a hieroglyphic birthday message and you have to use an F if you're writing Frankie and F is annoyingly one of the snakes."

"Oh," says Gran. "But not all snakes have scales, dear. What about the fluffy one by my front door that I use to keep out draughts?"

"I don't think ancient Egyptians had an Elmo, Gran."

"But Cleopatra would have loved him. She adored snakes! And I've just had a good idea. Why don't you invent your own hieroglyphics from symbols that you like?"

"Invent my own? That sounds brilliant!"

"Good," chuckles Gran. "Now I hear you have a job at the Deli and won't be coming to see me next week. I think I should like to work there. They wear nice stripy aprons and it'd be a whole lot better than my first job. I had to rake hay and it was very itchy, but lots of fun. First jobs always are. But I'm going to miss you so how about meeting up tomorrow? I could take you to the History Museum and we'll learn a bit more about ANCIENT EGYPT. It might help with the Cipher."

"Mmmm," I reply, trying to sound excited. "Thanks, Gran. I'll speak to Mum and check if it's OK."

"Lovely, dear."

And I cross my fingers and fib, "It'll be lots of fun.

But not as much fun as making up my own *hieroglyphics*! I think I'm going to get started now!"

"Lovely," repeats Gran.

And I say goodbye and take a look at the real *hieroglyphics*. And when I imagine the snakes as Elmo they instantly make me smile. But not as much as Gran's other idea! My own *hieroglyphics*! They can be mine and Frankie's own secret language.

Mum and Spike have gone to town so I rush to tell Dad who's working outside on his motorbike. I skip down the concrete steps and who should be skipping up, but Tiffany Me-Me.

"Hi, Minnie," she says. "I'm sorry about Dot's book."

"It's OK," I sigh. "She told me it was Otis who took it."

"Oh," says Tiff. "Then would you like to come to my place? We could think of something fun to do."

"I can't," I tell her. "I'm already busy."

"Doing what?" she asks.

I don't want to tell her I'm inventing an alphabet, so I pretend I haven't heard her and skip on down the steps. When I get outside Dad is up to his elbows in grease, but he looks up as I shout, "Gran's just had a good idea."

"Sounds like Gran," he laughs.

"She's told me to invent my own *hieroglyphics* and I'm going to call them Minnieglyphics."

"Terrific," says Dad. "I'd come and help you, but I'll be a couple of hours getting this lot shipshape."

"Or motorbike shape," laughs Tiffany, who has maddeningly followed me. "It's all right, Mr Piper. I can help Minnie."

And I'm steam-coming-out-of-my-ears annoyed! Not only has Tiffany found out my secret, but Dad says, "Great."

And it absolutely WON'T be great so I yawn, "It's OK, Tiff, you'd find it boring."

"Not if you offer her some of your Psychodelicious sweets," suggests Dad. "Sweets make everything very UNboring."

And I cannot believe he's just said that! But Tiffany's now even keener than ever and before I know it she's in my room, sitting on one of my furry beanbags and kicking off her high-heeled boots. I'm just thinking that they're almost exactly like the ones the girl in the sweet shop was wearing, when she says I can try them on. And they're so nice that even though I'm cross, I slip them on my feet and spookily they fit.

"Have a walk," bosses Tiff, and for once I obey and nearly fall over! "It's all down to practice," says Tiff. "Why don't you keep them on whilst we're doing Minnieglyphics?"

And it's probably a ploy to win me over, but I'm so desperate to stay in her boots that before I know it I'm hobbling to fetch some paper and pens. I suggest she invents her own Tiffanyglyphics and I'll do Minnieglyphics. But she looks at me blankly so I scribble the alphabet on a sheet of paper and next to A I doodle one of her boots. And next to B I draw the other boot facing in the opposite direction.

"Draw a different item for each letter," I tell her, "and then we can use them to write secret messages. These will be mine."

But typically Tiff copies me and draws her boots, too! This is have-to-grit-my-teeth annoying as I wanted Minnieglyphics to be unique and especially mine and definitely not Tiff's. So I tell her I will think of things I like and she must think of things she likes.

"OK," agrees Tiff, as Wanda comes to join us.

Then we both draw Wanda for C!

"Why don't we sit back to back," I sigh, "and then we can't see what the other's doodling?" And I turn around to stare out of my window, and Tiff faces my dressing table.

Then I look up at the sky and think it is gravity-defyingly peculiar that Dot is somewhere up there now. And I have no idea how planes stay up and rain doesn't, but I draw Dot for D, a plane for E, a cloud for F and raindrops for G. Then I imagine myself working at Minelli's Deli and draw all the pizzas I'm going to top and give each a pattern made from olives and tomatoes. Then P, Q and R are paper umbrellas that I'll pop in the top of milkshakes and smoothies, and S and T are stripy straws to schlurp them up. And U and V are strawberries and marshmallows to float on top! But I still haven't finished so I draw three ice creams, and I imagine I've squirted chocolate sauce on top, and with a felt pen I pretend-drizzle a funky palm tree and an Egyptian eye and a pyramid. And it takes for ever, but just as my fingers are dropping off I doodle Spike for Z and have finished.

"All done," I say to Tiff.

"And me! Have you written me a message, Minnie?"

"Not yet."

"I've nearly finished yours."

"That's good. I can't wait to read it." And I stare at her boots and get a toe-tinglingly brilliant idea! Excitedly I scribble:

Which is Minnieglyphics for SWAP YOU MY CLOGS FOR YOUR BOOTS JUST FOR ONE NIGHT. And I hand it to Tiff, along with my sheet of Minnieglyphics.

Tiff hands me

along with her Tiffanyglyphics, written in my very best glitter pen.

I'm just about to start decoding when Tiff says, "All this thinking's making me hungry, Minnie." And she's staring at my dressing table and my Psychodelicious bag of sweets.

I now wish I'd made her face the window, but it's too late and I try to sound chirpy as I say, "Shall we have some sweets then?"

"If you don't mind," says Tiff.

I DO mind. I EXTREMELY mind. But I think of the secret message I've scribbled and she's much more likely to lend me her boots if I've been really nice.

So, like a giddy giraffe I shuffle to my dressing table and cross my fingers that none of my hidden goody bag of Pyramids have fallen out from behind the mirror. I definitely don't want to part with those! But thankfully they haven't and I catch a glimpse of myself in the mirror and I have to grin because my legs look just like the girl's in the sweet shop!

This puts me in a better mood and I confidently smile as I offer Tiff my sweets. Tiffany interprets this as please-take-absolutely-as-many-as-you-like, and only leaves me the already opened packet of LOVEHEARTS and one tube of VIOLETS. I stare at the VIOLETS and wonder how something that looks so delicious and is lavender-purple, my favourite colour, could possibly taste quite so disgusting. And as I don't want to eat them I decide to save them as a lucky charm and totter to my bed to pop them on my pillow. And they're already working because I'm walking better! And then Tiffany says I look really pretty and in a smiley mood I set about cracking her secret message. But it's not as easy as you might think because there are twenty-six different symbols and it's not until I get my third '**T**' that I realize I need to check for multiples. Repetitively brilliantly there are four more '**E**'s and two more '**R**'s and now I'm decoding like a true undercover puzzler. But suddenly my smile drops as I read...

THANK YOU FOR LETTING ME BE YOUR BEST FRIEND

Tiffany is NOT my best friend! But she's cracked my message and maddeningly I realize that best friends swap shoes, and she's staring at my clogs saying, "Can I borrow your glitter pen, too?"

And this is typical of Tiff. She always wants more and it's why Frankie is my best friend and Tiffany Me-Me is not. But I look at her boots and the PARMA VIOLETS and picture myself as the girl in the sweet shop. And before I can say that's-what-friends-are-for I am handing her my clogs and pen.

"Promise me you'll look after them?"

"Promise," beams Tiff. "Best friend's promise."

## SATURDAY NIGHT

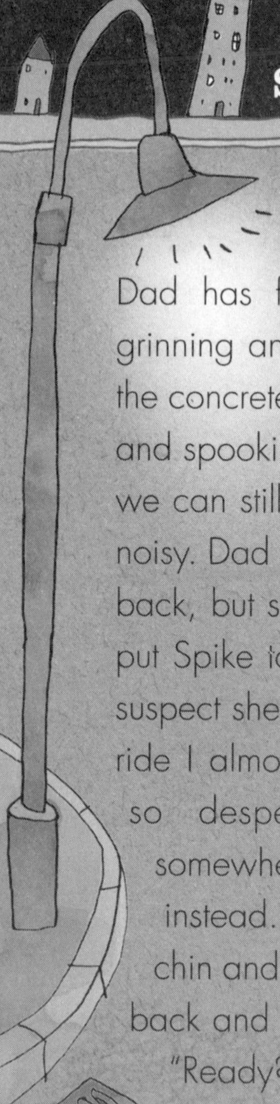

### Mind-bogglingly tricky

Dad has finished his motorbike! He is non-stop grinning and me, Mum and Spike all traipse down the concrete steps to go and take a look. It's bedtime and spookily dark, but the street lights are shining so we can still see it and it's black and silver and very noisy. Dad looks proud and offers Mum a ride on the back, but she shakes her head and says she has to put Spike to bed as it's getting very late. Truthfully I suspect she's scared and when Dad asks if I'd like a ride I almost say it's my bedtime too. But he looks so desperate to take somebody somewhere that I fetch my helmet instead. Dad fastens it under my chin and nervously I climb on the back and hold on tight.

"Ready?" he laughs.

"Ready!" I gulp.

And suddenly the bike is moving and we're off round Arthurs Way!

It's zippily exciting and not nearly as scary as I thought it would be and going round corners is especially fun because we have to lean over and sit back up and Dad says I'm a bit of a natural. It's like being on a fairground ride and I'd like to stay on longer but Dad says we'd better get home.

"I'll drive you to the Deli on Monday," he says.

"Thanks!" I smile, and I really mean it. Monday's going to be SOOOO exciting! Dad chains the bike to a lamp post and we head back to the flat.

Miraculously Spike is snoring and Mum is taking a quiet moment to calm herself with yoga. I kiss her goodnight and clean my teeth and skip off to my bedroom. The PARMA VIOLETS are still on my pillow and I cross my fingers that they'll bring me luck as I climb into my PJs and TIFFANY'S BOOTS!! Mum wouldn't let me wear them earlier as she said they'd stop my toes from growing. But what she can't see she won't know and I'm so desperate to keep wearing them that in bed is better than nothing. Then I cover them with the duvet so she won't see them and set about deciphering the keyword:

The confusing thing about *hieroglyphics* is that some letters have the same symbol. F, J and V are all snakes and I, E and Y are reeds, but luckily the keyword doesn't contain any of these and I'm soon discovering that = U, = T, = E, = A, = M and = L. Which hieroglyphically brilliantly means the keyword is **UTEAML**! The only trouble is that **UTEAML** is not a word I've ever heard of, but Mr Impey said that the person who invents the code can use any word they fancy so I scribble out the alphabet and under A to F, I line up **UTEAML**. And the last letter of the keyword is **L** so the next letter in the cipher has to be **M**. But I've already used this so I move on to **N**. Then **O**. Then **P**. And eventually I have

A B C D E F G H I J K L M N O P Q R S T U V W X Y Z
U T E A M L N O P Q R S V W X Y Z B C D F G H I J K

At last I'm ready to crack the message, but first I need to turn

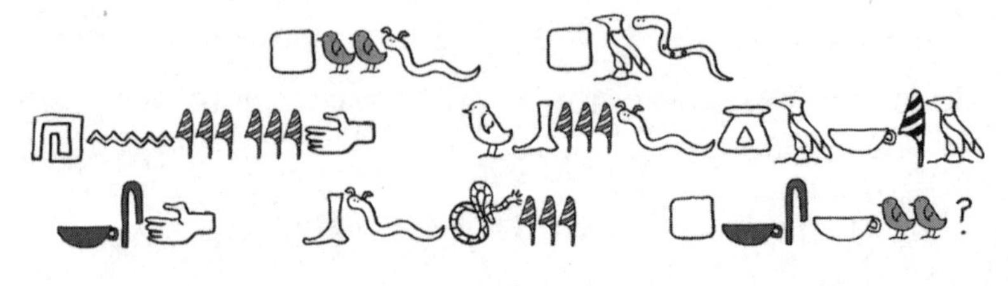

into English. It's brain-scramblingly fiddly, but eventually I doodle PWF PAJ HNEED UBEFGAKIA XD BFOE PXKW?, which means, at last, I can start decoding. I find the first letter, P, in the Cipher line and look for the letter above it, I. I scribble it down and then hunt for W and above it is N. And above F is U. INU. This doesn't seem right, but perhaps Cleopatra has put the spaces between the letters in the wrong place. Maybe she's even done it on purpose to make it mind-bogglingly tricky! If this is the case the first word could be IN, and the second word start with U.

My alien pen whizzes back and forth between the two lines and finally, I hold up my notebook and struggle to read INU IDY WGCCT ARCUVDZXD OT RUHC IOZN? But I can't recognize any words even if I change the spacing. It might as well be written in ancient Egyptian so the keyword must be wrong. But if it isn't UTEAML what is it? My brain aches and my toes are beginning to pinch in Tiff's boots and it's hard to think when both ends of your body hurt.

And then Dad sneaks in and giggles, "I'm glad you like my motorbike, Minnie!"

"I love it," I grin. "I wish solving codes was just as much fun."

"But I thought you liked solving codes?"

"I do usually, but not this one. I can't find the keyword."

"I expect it's locked in your brain somewhere! Locked … get it. KEYword."

"That's terrible," I sigh.

"Not as terrible as Mum's caterpillar smoothies!" says Dad. And he disappears clutching his stomach and I shake my head that is spinning with motorbikes, keywords and caterpillars, and there is no space left for Chocolate Ciphers. I decide to give up and tap on my wall for Wanda Wellingtons and she trots in and sits on my rug. She's in her Sphinx pose and waiting for me to pat my duvet.

"Do you think you're Egyptian?" I giggle.

Wanda nods and wags her tail and I pat my duvet three times and she jumps up and licks my face as if it might be made out of chocolate.

"I've been on a motorbike," I whisper. And Wanda's ears twitch and she curls up in a ball at my feet and we both fall fast asleep.

## SUNDAY DAY

### Lucky charms

Gran is taking me to the museum today and I was hoping to make it more fun by wearing Tiffany's boots. But Mum says no and that I must take them back on my way to Gran's. And I don't want to tell her that I'm nervous about meeting Otis and Presley so I pull on my hoody and wave goodbye.

But Mum fusses, "That hoody's very grubby, Minnie. And you haven't brushed your hair."

"It's dark in museums," I mumble back. "No one will see me. And anyway, the only people there will be short-sighted boffins." And before she can moan about anything else I head off to Tiff's. As soon as I'm outside I pull on the boots and I'm so desperate to keep wearing them that, although Tiff lives on the floor below me, I walk down two flights of steps, up again and back down one. And then I cannot believe it but I pass Tiffany's parents. Mrs Mead can't walk very well and

Mr Mead is pushing her in her wheelchair towards the lift. I smile nervously and hope they won't notice I'm hobbling in their daughter's shoes, but just in case, I totter quickly to Flat 27 and knock nervously on Tiffany's door.

Just as I feared Otis opens it and growls, "What do YOU want, Piper?"

"Is Tiffany in, please?" I ask.

"Maybe," he grunts, but Tiffany has heard me and pushes past him, and as she does he trips her up and one of my clogs comes flying off. Tyson snatches it and Otis guffaws and when Tiffany rescues it it's dripping with slobber just like the dog.

"Sorry," says Tiff.

And so am I. I want to remind her about promising to look after them, but it was a best friend's promise, and I don't want to go there, so I take off her boots and Otis snatches them and tosses them to Presley. Presley flings them back to Otis and Tiffany shouts, "Me, ME, give them to ME!" But her brothers don't listen and Otis jumps on her and I want to tell him to leave her alone. But Tyson is growling and threatening to pounce if I dare just to whisper.

I need to get out of here before Tyson gobbles me up and bravely I ask, "Can I have my clogs and glitter pen please, Tiff?"

"No!" laughs Otis, and hurls me Tiffany's boots instead. Then he hollers, "Fetch!" and scarily Tyson is charging my way and the only thing I can think to do is toss the boots over the balcony. Tyson hurtles past me and down the steps on a mission to get them back.

"Idiot!" shouts Otis. "If he runs off it's YOUR fault, Piper." And he and Presley scarper after him.

Tiffany mumbles, "They broke your glitter pen, Minnie. But I'll buy you a new one."

"Don't worry," I sigh. "It was just a pen."

"Thanks," says Tiff. "You're a best friend."

"Just a friend," I tell her. "Frankie's my best friend."

"But Frankie isn't here," reminds Tiff. And she hands me the clogs and mumbles, "I'd better help get Tyson back. Dad will go crazy if we've let him escape."

And I hastily make my own escape, and I do not look back until I get to Gran's.

☆ ☆ ☆

I'm so relieved when Gran opens her door.

"Hello, Minnie," she cheers, beckoning me in. "How are you getting on with the Chocolate Cipher?"

"Not great," I tell her. "It's hard to concentrate because Spike keeps crying."

"Poor Spike," says Gran. "Teething can be a painful business."

"It certainly hurts my ears," I groan.

"You could always drown him out with some music," she offers.

"Maybe, but I need it quiet when I'm deciphering puzzles. Especially tricky ones where you have to find a keyword. I've brought it with me. Would you like to see it?"

"Yes, please," beams Gran.

And I unfold the Cipher and explain how I found UTEAML. "But it's not right," I sigh, "and now I don't know what to do next."

"Hmmmm," says Gran. "Perhaps you should try another part of the puzzle. It might be easier to crack."

"But I need the keyword. It's cryptically important in keyword Ciphers. Without it I can't read Cleopatra's message."

"But if you can't find it you need to move on to a different part. What about this, dear?" And she points to the very last line of the puzzle.

"OK," I sigh. And I stare at [hieroglyphs] and twiddle the PARMA VIOLETS in my hoody pocket and realize that I haven't yet turned these hieroglyphics into anything I can read! I look at the deCipher sheet and confidently scribble GOOD LUCK.

"Good luck!" I shout to Gran. "The last line spells good luck! My PARMA VIOLETS must be working."

"I didn't know you liked PARMA VIOLETS," says Gran.

"I don't," I tell her. "I just have them to bring me luck and make me more confident. They're supposed to be my lucky charm."

"Your amulet," smiles Gran.

"What's an amulet?" I ask.

"I'll show you, dear. I thought this book would come in handy." And she opens a book called EVERYTHING YOU NEED TO KNOW ABOUT ANCIENT EGYPT and points to a page headed AMULETS. And they're truthfully really tiny carvings and most are beetles, but some are eyes and some are men with creatures' heads. And a caption reads: "The Egyptians wore them to bring them good luck."

There it is again! GOOD LUCK!

"So an amulet's a lucky charm!" I exclaim.

"Just like your PARMA VIOLETS," says Gran. "And now you're feeling lucky I think you should reread this." And she points to

DECODE AND UNSCRAMBLE: .

Decode and unscramble. Unscramble.

"I've not been unscrambling!" I splutter. "I've decoded but the letters are scrambled and in the wrong order! They're an anagram and that's why the Cipher didn't work."

And I stare at the PARMA VIOLETS and the words GOOD LUCK and suddenly I have my keyword! UTEAML unscrambled spells...

"Amulet!" I squeal to Gran. "The keyword is AMULET!"

"Goodness," says Gran. "How lucky is that! And the History Museum is full of them."

"Really?" I smile.

"I thought today would be lucky," beams Gran. And she fetches her coat and we're off.

☆ ☆ ☆

The museum is nowhere near as boring as I thought it would be and, even though I'm in a dark room, I haven't fallen asleep. Gran and I are studying a mummy in a casket and it's a dead person wrapped in bandages and I have a spooky feeling that I should be scared, but peculiarly I'm not. The Egyptians were very excited about death and believed when you died you went to a place called the Netherworld and the Sun God, Ra, visited you and a Goddess, Nephthys, watched over you. They decorated the caskets with gods and goddesses and wrote prayers and spells in *hieroglyphics* to protect the dead in the afterlife.

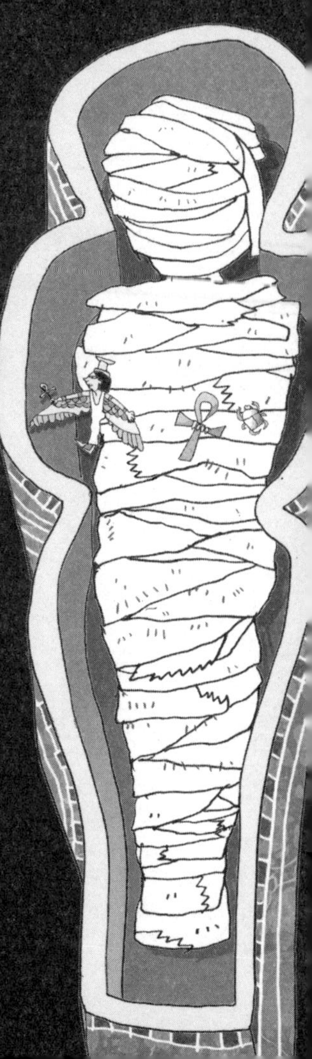

"I think that's a statue of Nephthys," says Gran, pointing to a carving tucked in the casket. "And look! There are lots of…"

"Amulets!" I exclaim. "The mummy has amulets inside her coffin."

"To bring her good luck in the Netherworld," says Gran. "The Egyptians thought the Netherworld was just like the real world and that the dead needed money, food and pets. Sometimes they only buried pictures or models, but often it was the real thing. Look, there's a mummified cat."

"They used to bury their real pets?!" I exclaim.

"Sometimes," nods Gran. "The Egyptians were very fond of cats. But they weren't buried in holes in the ground. They were entombed in magnificent pyramids. And d'you know why they were called pyramids, dear?"

I shake my head and Gran says, "A type of Egyptian cake was called a Pyramis and was pyramid shaped and they were probably named after this."

"That's amazing!" I tell her. "You're so clever."

"Actually, I just read it on this plaque!" she giggles.

"Cheat!" I exclaim. "But if the Egyptians called their tombs after a cake, maybe we should call our graves doughnuts!"

"Now that does sound delicious, dear. Shall we nip to the café and see if they sell them? I could just do with a grave."

"And me!" I giggle. And we climb the stairs in the corner of the museum and while I find an empty table Gran joins the queue. Then I look up to see how she's doing, and I cannot believe it, but there in front of her is … the wish-I-could-be-confident-like-her girl from Psychodelicious! And she looks cooler than ever and is laughing and talking to Abhi Talwar. Abhi Talwar from my class! She must be his girlfriend!

Abhi is tall and grown up and clever and I'm not surprised she thinks he's nice. He's almost as cute as Nero Minelli and suddenly he's staring at me and smiling a big, wide grin. I try to smile back, but I'm instantly aware that my hair is like a nest for sparrows, and my hoody's stained with caterpillar smoothie and I blush the colour of strawberry jam. I hadn't expected to see anyone I knew. Especially someone whose girlfriend looks so cool. She's in a funky purple dress and pointy boots and I'm in a splattered top.

I have a desperate urge to disappear, but they buy their drinks and wander over to my table.

"Hi, again!" smiles the girl.

And I cannot believe she's remembered me, and I am just worrying if it's because I look odd when Abhi says, "Hi, Minnie. Have you solved the Cipher yet?"

"A bit," I splutter. But I can't think about hieroglyphics. I can only think about my hair and hoody.

"How about the wordsearch? I've chosen pyramids..."

And I haven't a clue what he's on about so I stupidly blurt, "Can you tell Gran I've gone to the loo?"

"OK," shrugs Abhi.

And I stand up, but embarrassingly realize that now they'll see my jeans as well. And they're horridly baggy in all the wrong places and my clogs are covered in Tyson's slobber so ridiculously I sit back down. "I ... I ... I think I can wait," I stammer. "Oh, look, here's Gran."

Abhi and the girl say hi to Gran and move away to a nearby table. I feel very silly and if the girl didn't think I was odd before, she definitely will do now because Gran hands me a chocolate doughnut and says, "I hope you enjoy your grave, dear!"

The girl's ears twitch and suddenly I have lost my appetite. It takes me for ever to swallow the doughnut, and thankfully Abhi and his girlfriend finish before me and when they leave and say goodbye I cross my fingers that they go straight home. Gran's keen to nip to the museum shop and I hope they won't be in there, too.

Luckily they're not and Gran buys herself a tea towel with a recipe for Pyramis cake printed on it and a chocolate sphinx for me. I buy a gold scarab amulet for Frankie as a present to go with her Chocolate Pyramids.

When we get back to Gran's she lends me her book on ANCIENT EGYPT and I run home as fast as I can to try and get started on the code. Finally I have my keyword, but as I reach my flat, there on the doorstep is a sheet of paper. It's a bit crumpled and I pick it up and can barely believe it, for on one side are Tiffanyglyphics and on the other is a scary secret message!

And it probably says, *Dear best friend*, or worse still, *Tyson hasn't come back and it's all your fault*. My heart sinks and with shaking fingers I bury the paper in Gran's book, clutch the PARMA VIOLETS in my pocket, and decide to never read it!

## SUNDAY NIGHT

### Girlfriends and gremlins

After tea of noodles and bean sprouts the phone rings and it's Frankie.

"Frankie?" I squeal. "How was Italy?"

"It was OK."

"Only OK?"

"There were too may aunties pinching my cheeks and telling me how I've grown. But never mind that. How was Cocoanuts?"

"The best!" I tell her. "We tried squillions of samples of yummy chocolate, and stood under giant palm trees with monkeys and coconuts hanging from their branches. And when you wound up a monkey's tail it sang Cocoanuts is nuts about cocoa!"

"Fabiozo!" laughs Frankie. "I wish I could have gone."

"But that's not all," I tell her. "There was an Egyptian room full of sand with a big gold pyramid and hieroglyphics carved in the walls. And the staff were dressed in togas and had black lines painted round their eyes.

And there was even a man in a hairnet called Brian Willy Wonka Wilson."

"Trust me to miss all that," sighs Frankie. "All I've had is Nero being moody the entire holiday because he's missing his new girlfriend."

"I didn't know he had a girlfriend!" I exclaim.

"Nor me," says Frankie. "Not until the holiday, but now he won't stop talking about her. I'm bored of her already and I haven't even met her yet."

"I wonder what she looks like?"

"A gremlin I expect. And she's bound to be smelly! I should bring a peg for your nose tomorrow because she's coming to the Deli."

"Abhi Talwar's got a girlfriend too!"

"Really?!" laughs Frankie. "Who'd ever want to go out with him?"

"Well, he's quite nice for a boy," I tell her. "And he's clever. He was analyzing the Chocolate Gold Pyramids and..."

"Chocolate what?" interrupts Frankie.

"Ooops! Nothing!" The chocolates were supposed to be a surprise!

"Tell me!" laughs Frankie.

"I'll tell you tomorrow." And I'm desperate to tell her about the Cipher too, but it will just have to wait.

Frankie giggles and says, "Did you miss me?"

"Of course I did. Everything was boring without you."

"And Tiffany Me-Me isn't your new best friend? *Me, me, me, Minnie, can I be your friend now Frankie's not here?*" And she has Tiffany's voice off to a tee and she hoots with laughter and I do not tell her that I borrowed Tiff's boots. Or that she borrowed my clogs and glitter pen. Or that we wrote secret messages and one's still hiding in Gran's book. "Don't be late tomorrow," she warns. "I don't want to be stuck with Nero's smelly gremlin."

"I won't," I promise. And then Mum hands me Spike to kiss goodnight and he hollers in my ear. "Perhaps I could swap you Spike for Nero?" I offer.

"Hmmmm?" laughs Frankie. "Oooh, got to go, Minnie. Dad's just baked a pizza!"

"You're so lucky!" I tell her. "I love pizzas and my tea was bean sprouts and noodles!"

But Frankie's not listening and puts down the phone. It was fun speaking to her and I'm so glad she's back but I feel a bit guilty about Tiffany. I know I haven't done anything bad, but Frankie might get the wrong end of the stick. Perhaps I should have told her that Tiff came over. But it's too late now and time for bed, so I go to my room and plan to tell her tomorrow. But tomorrow's her birthday and I don't want to upset her then, so I decide to keep quiet, at least until Tuesday. And to take my mind off feeling guilty I eat a Chocolate Pyramid instead! And I don't know if it's because it's Egyptian but I suddenly get a brainwave to make a mummy-shaped casket to put Frankie's presents in. The only trouble is that I'm supposed to be snoring and the cardboard I need is in the kitchen.

Luckily no one sees me tiptoe from my room or return with scissors and a muesli box. But making a casket is trickier than I thought and it doesn't exactly look authentic because muesli is from Switzerland and not ANCIENT EGYPT. But I paint it gold and it starts to look better, and then I decorate it with Minnieglyphics and a top secret message...

It's now starting to look realistically good and I remember back to the coffin in the museum and how it was decorated with gods and goddesses. I doodle

the Sun God, Ra, on the lid bobbing about in his boat in the Netherworld. Then I look in Gran's book to find out how to draw the Goddess Nephthys. It says an evil god killed her brother, Osiris, so she magicked herself into a kite to hover over his body to protect him. How cool is that? And it gives me an even cooler idea! I'll make Frankie a Nephthys kite!

I unwrap the tissue paper from the scarab I bought at the History Museum and snip it into a kite shape. Then to one end I tie a length of thread and attach eight tissue bows and on each I scribble a Minnieglyphic letter and secretly spell Nephthys! I try to fly it and it nearly works if I blow quite hard and then I nestle it artistically on top of the scarab and ten Chocolate Gold Pyramids. The casket now looks truthfully Egyptian and I can't wait to give it to Frankie. But as I close Gran's book a crumpled piece of paper falls out – Tiffany's secret message! And I know I wasn't going to read it, but somehow I can't help it. I wriggle deeper undercover, unwrap the sphinx that Gran bought me, and with secret chocolate lips, and panic in my heart, I set about deciphering.

TO MY BEST FRIEND MINNIE
I'M SORRY ABOUT YOUR
GLITTER PEN.
I'LL BUY YOU A NEW ONE IN
TOWN TOMORROW.
LET'S MEET ON TUESDAY AND
I'LL GIVE IT TO YOU THEN.
TIFF
X

# MONDAY DAY

## Smelly Lavender

Dad takes me to Frankie's on his motorbike! It's much more fun than travelling by bus and as he pulls up in front of the Deli, he gives me a wink as I run inside. The café smells of coffee, and Frankie is munching a croissant at the counter. But as soon as she sees me she jumps up.

"You look like a spaceman!" giggles Frankie.

I do a twirl in my crash helmet and hand her her present and then Nero bounds in with a girl by his side.

"Hi, Minnie," he says. "This is Lavender."

"She's Nero's girlfriend," whispers Frankie.

But she isn't Nero's girlfriend. She's ABHI'S girlfriend! It's the wish-I-could-be-like-her girl! And she's called Lavender, my favourite colour!

"Hi, Minnie," she smiles. "We obviously like the same places!"

"H-h-hi," I stammer back.

And she's still acting confidently, even though she knows I saw her with Abhi! My knees would be shaking, but Lavender's knees are as cool as a cucumber in purple tights and high-heeled boots. And she has a funky hat pulled over one of her eyes and I have a space helmet pulled over mine. I yank it off and the top of my hair is squashed flat and I feel a bit like Brian Willy Wonka Wilson when he whisked off his hairnet.

I flush scarlet and think Frankie was right when she called her a smelly gremlin yesterday. How could anyone two-time Nero? He's the dreamiest boy on the planet.

But before I can say anything Fabio comes out of the kitchen and says, "I'm so happy you could all help." And he hands us a plate of hot croissants and they're flakily delicious and so much nicer than my breakfast at home which was pumpkin seeds and yoghurt. "Nero and Lavender," he says, "your jobs this morning are to make the coffees and take orders from the customers. Frankie and Minnie, you can help in the kitchen."

"Cool," smiles Lavender.

And that's just what she is, confident and cool. But whilst Nero's been in Italy she's been two-timing him with Abhi! One day Abhi, the next Nero. I have to tell Frankie, but she's busily tearing the paper off her present.

"Thanks, Minnie!" she screeches, as she whisks the lid off the casket. The kite's wedged inside it, which she doesn't notice, and the foil around one of the Pyramids is damaged, but other than that it still looks nice.

"Chocolate Gold Pyramids!" coos Lavender.

"They're a brand new sort of sweet," I tell Frankie. "I got them from Cocoanuts and they're dreamily delicious. Hardly anyone has tried them yet."

"I have!" says Lavender. "And Minnie's right. They are delicious."

And I'm gnash-my-teeth annoyed that this gremlin has tried one before Frankie. Abhi must have given it to her! And I'm about to confront her when Frankie bites the top off a Pyramid and caramel oozes over her lips. "I look like Mrs Elliott!" she giggles.

"Who's Mrs Elliott?" asks Fabio.

"Dot's teacher," she grins. "She's got a brown moustache!"

And we all laugh and she goes back to my present and takes out the amulet. "Fabiozo, Minnie!"

"It's an amulet," I tell her. "To bring you good luck!"

"I need it!" laughs Frankie, staring at Nero.

The gremlin slyly peeks at the casket, but she probably, definitely doesn't like it because she doesn't say anything and then a bell chimes and the Deli door opens and people start coming in.

"Chop, chop!" winks Fabio, and Nero jumps up and Lavender follows him. Then they smile at the customers and ask politely what they would like.

"You two can practise clearing tables," says Fabio, grinning at me and Frankie.

We scoop up the croissant plate and brush the crumbs on to it and follow Fabio into the kitchen. He kits us out with aprons and I think of Gran and her first job of raking hay in the fields.

"I'd like you to grate this cheese for me, please," says Fabio. "And empty these olives into that tub."

Frankie reaches for a grater and I tip out the olives, and then we both wash a bag of peppers, tomatoes and lettuce. The water sprays everywhere and it's a good job we're wearing aprons.

"What do you think of Lavender?" whispers Frankie.

"She's..."

"Not a smelly gremlin!" laughs Frankie. "I can't believe anyone as Fabaroony as her would see anything in my brother."

And I'm just wondering if I should say Lavender also sees something in Abhi Talwar when Frankie gushes, "And she's SOOOOO nice! She even bought me a birthday present. My first bouquet of flowers. And she tied them with lavender ribbon and they made me feel all kind of grown up." And I suddenly panic that my home-made casket is a babyish gift. No wonder Lavender didn't comment! But Frankie adds, "Not as cool as your present though, Minnie. Now I don't feel so bad for having missed out on Cocoanuts."

And I'm not sure if she's just saying this, but I try to believe her and mumble, "Trevor and Jasen didn't go either. Trevor's got the mumps."

"Serves him right!" laughs Frankie.

"Maybe. But he did try hard to be good in the end. He was even nice to me and Dot..."

"Trevor, nice?"

"Well, nicer than normal. He rescued us from Otis and Presley." And while we knead the dough for the lunchtime pizzas I tell her about Tyson and Wanda in the park.

I've never kneaded dough before, but it's actually just about squashing and punching and Frankie divides hers into three balls and says, "This ball is Otis and this is Tyson and this is Presley!" And when she punches them I copy her exactly and Fabio says we look like experts and gives us badges saying, "Fantastico Pizza Maker".

Then we press the dough into circles and Fabio pronounces them pizza-perfect and can we make twenty more?

"OK," we giggle, and pizza making is totally fun and we spoon lashings of tomato sauce on the bases and sprinklings of grated mozzarella cheese and wait for the orders to roll in.

By lunchtime the Deli is queuing-back-to-the-door busy and we get to add the extra toppings. Some want basil, and some want mushrooms or ham or salami, and soon I'm learning what the names mean when Fabio shouts, "Two Margaritas!" which is tomato and cheese, "Two Milano!" which is peppers and ham, and "One Minelli Special!" which means heaps of absolutely everything!

We are allowed to nibble all morning, but at two o'clock we have a late lunch. We all tuck into Minelli Specials and everyone wants to know about Cocoanuts.

"There was a jungle room," I tell them, "with giant palm trees and singing monkeys and an Egyptian room full of sand and a shiny gold pyramid bigger than Mr Impey made out of lots of Chocolate Gold Pyramids. And we watched machines wrap up sweets and the staff wore hairnets or togas!"

"I wish I'd gone," says Nero.

"And me," says Fabio.

"And me," echoes Lavender.

"And you got to try all those chocolates!" says Frankie.

"I know," I grin. "Zingy chilli, fruity raspberry, spicy orange and would-like-it-as-toothpaste breath-fresh peppermint. When I grow up I'm going to get a job as a chocolate tester!"

Nero swoons. "Does somebody really have that job?"

And I can't believe he's swooning at me and I'm about to tell him about Cleopatra, when Lavender says, "I'm going to be a fashion designer when I leave school."

And my face sags because being a fashion designer is probably cooler than being a chocolate tester. And I'm just feeling silly when Nero says, "Minnie's parents are both designers."

"They are?" I splutter.

"Of course!" laughs Frankie. "Interior designers. Who else has got an orange spotty good-manners-teaching table!"

"I've never really thought about it," I mumble. And I truthfully haven't, but now I come to think about it, our flat is different from everyone else's.

"And Minnie's mum's painting a mural in a flower shop," adds Nero.

"Wow!" says Lavender. "Your mum must be cool!"

And I'm about to tell her that Mum is definitely not cool when Frankie grins and says, "Minnie's really artistic too. Look at these pictures she's drawn on my casket." And she opens it again and squeals, "There's a kite in the lid!"

"That's the Goddess Nephthys," I tell her.

"*Fabaroony!*" laughs Frankie. "I love goddesses!"

"That's because you are one," says Fabio. "A birthday goddess."

"I love goddesses, too," says Lavender. "Especially Saraswati. She's the Hindu goddess of art."

And like a gremlin she's butting in again and I worry her goddess is better than mine, so I add, "Nephthys's name is secretly hidden in the kite's tails. And that's the Sun God, Ra, in his boat," and I point at my painting on the top of the casket.

Lavender studies it and I am giddily shocked when she says, "This casket is awesome, Minnie. And I love the *hieroglyphics*."

"They're not *hieroglyphics*," I tell her. "They're Minnieglyphics."

"Crazy!" says Nero. "What do they say?"

"It's a secret," I tell him. "A secret message from me to Frankie in our very own language." And I hand Frankie a scribbled copy of my Minnieglyphic alphabet.

"*Fabaroony!*" she squeals. "I'm going to read it

NOW!" And she immediately tries to decipher it but she's hopeless at codes and says, "Someone's going to have to help me or I'll be here all week!"

"I'll help!" says Lavender.

And I completely panic. Lavender must definitely NOT read the message! "But then it won't be a secret," I splutter. "I'll help you later, Frankie, but I think we'd better tidy up or Fabio will be cross."

"Then let him be cross!" giggles Frankie. "Don't forget it's my birthday!"

And my heart races as she and Lavender huddle together and stare at

And together they read

FINGERS CROSSED THIS AMULET WILL BRING YOU LOTS OF GOOD LUCK AND NERO'S GIRLFRIEND WON'T BE...

"Ooh, what won't I be?" giggles Lavender.

And I try to grab the paper but Frankie holds it tight and together they decipher the last word –

SSSSSS SMELLY!

Me and Frankie both blush, but Lavender remains as confident as ever. "Well am I?" she laughs.

"Of course not!" says Frankie.

And she fragrantly isn't. Just a hint of lavender, true to her name. But how can a girl who looks so nice, and a girl that I've been trying to copy, actually be so horrid? And she keeps making me feel really silly and I absolutely have to tell Frankie that she's a two-timing gremlin. But I can't do it now with everyone here. And then the door chimes and we look up and it's Delilah and Tallulah. They both want identical Knickerbocker Glories and Fabio asks me and Frankie to make them. Soon we are layering up Malteasers and chopped banana and toffee ice cream and topping it with a squirt of cream.

"Don't forget the sauce," reminds Tallulah. And I know it's Tallulah because her hair-bobble's pink and this gives me a fun idea and with the pink raspberry sauce I squiggle a T on Tallulah's, and in purply blackcurrant sauce I doodle D on Delilah's.

The twins think this is deliciously brilliant and Frankie says, "Tomorrow we should have our own

Knickerbocker Glories with F and M squiggled on the top! But in our own secret language!"

I can hardly wait and I think about what flavour I shall have all afternoon. And I can't decide between toffee, vanilla, mint-choc chip or raspberry, and I think of Lavender and how she'd just know what flavour would be best. And I cross my fingers and plump for double chocolate ice cream with marshmallows and strawberries. Then, while I'm in a deciding mood, I double-check that Nero's not around, sidle up to Frankie and resolve NOW is the time to tell her my secret. And I'm just whispering, "Frankie I've got something to tell you..." when Fabio appears with a chocolate cake and eleven silver candles.

"Surprise!" giggles Nero, following behind him.

Frankie is speechless and so am I.

Lavender starts singing "Happy Birthday" and we all join in and Frankie looks so happy that I cannot spoil her special moment. My secret must wait.

But I look at the gremlin and think to myself, "Tomorrow is another day!"

## MONDAY EVENING

# NO DOGS

Dad is jealous that I had a Minelli Special pizza for lunch because all he had was a watercress sandwich. "Can you smuggle some home, Minnie?" he whispers, holding his nose as Mum chops up six cloves of garlic.

"I'll try," I whisper back. "What's for tea?"

"Something smelly," giggles Dad.

"I heard that, Malcolm," says Mum. "Garlic is good for you."

"Not if you're a vampire," says Dad. "Or you have to kiss the Queen."

"Which means you're safe," says Mum. "Now lay the table and try to be useful."

I run to my room in case she asks me to do something, too, because I've got no time for chopping onions or peeling potatoes. I need to get cracking with the Chocolate Cipher. There always seems to be something to distract me like writing secret messages to Frankie, solving secret messages from Tiff, or taking Wanda and Dot for walks. So I sneak into bed and try to hide with my code and *hieroglyphics*. And I've just flicked on my alien pen when Wanda joins me beneath my duvet and is non-stop fidgeting.

"Hello, Wanda," I whisper. "Can you sit still because I've got something important to decipher."

But Wanda ignores me and licks my ears, which means it's impossible to doodle the alphabet without going wonky. Underneath it I print AMULET followed by all the other letters of the alphabet that I haven't used, trying to make sure that the letters line up, which isn't easy as everything is skew-whiff and Wanda is sticking her tail up my nostrils! I am just checking I can still read it when Mum says, "Could you take Wanda for her walk please, Minnie, before it gets dark."

Wanda's ears prick up and she bounces out of bed and tugs at my duvet. "I'm sure spies never have this trouble," I grumble. "They probably have perfect peace when they need to decipher secret codes." But I crawl out of bed and bundle the cipher into my pocket and Wanda runs off to fetch her lead and waits by the door.

We don't go to the park because I'm nervous that Otis and Presley will be there, so instead we head to the local shops. Wanda loves the shops, especially the butcher's, and when we get there her nose twitches and her tail wags, even though the butcher's is closed. She knows it's where we get her bones and ogles the sign saying BOTTOMLEY'S BUTCHERS. And now she has read it, and is doggily sure that she's in the right place, she jumps up at the window and barks.

"It's closed," I tell her. "Mr Bottomley's gone home for his tea and is probably munching sausages with Trevor. I expect it's why Trevor draws sausages so well, even if they're supposed to be intestines. He has them every night for his tea."

Wanda's speciality is devouring sausages and she jumps even higher as if trying to bounce her way in. I pick her up and say, "Look! Mr Bottomley and his sausages aren't there!" And I feel slightly uncomfortable because there's a security camera pointing right at me and on a sticker in the window it says, WARNING – THESE PREMISES ARE PROTECTED BY CCTV.

I shuffle away and gaze into the shop next door, which is BUBBLES Launderette. It's still open and, while the machines are churning the washing, people are sitting peacefully with absolutely nothing to do. No one is bothering them and I clutch my lucky PARMA VIOLETS in my pocket and sigh, "I wish I could do that. I wish I had a space where no one bothered me." And I'm just wondering if Wanda would behave in the launderette, and would let me sit there and puzzle for a bit, when I notice a sign saying NO DOGS. That rules that idea out, but then I get another one and whisper, "What if I tie you up outside, Wanda, and you stare at Mr Bottomley's shop and I stare at the code?!"

Wanda seems to like this idea and jumps from my arms and immediately trots back to the butcher's. I tie her to the lamp post and say, "I'll be in BUBBLES."

And I point my finger at the launderette and then sneak inside and invent a plan that if anyone asks me what I'm doing I'll say I'm waiting for Mum, who's gone home to fetch more washing. And it's a truthful-sounding plan, but nobody asks, and nobody bothers me, and happily I open my notebook and beneath the alphabet and Cipher I print Cleopatra's secret message...

alphabet = A B C D E F G H I J K L M N O P Q R S T U V W X Y Z
cipher = A M U L E T V W X Y Z B C D F G H I J K N O P Q R S

secret message = PWF PAJ HNEED UBEFGAKIA XD BFOE PXKW?

Now for the exciting bit! I take the first letter of the message, P, and look for it in the Cipher. Immediately above it is W which I scribble down and finally I'm deCiphering! I glance at Wanda and she's still dreaming about sausages, so I progress to letter two, which is Wanda's initial, W. I find it in the Cipher and above it is H. WH! The next letter's bound to be Y because I know the Cipher is a question as it ends with a question mark and most questions start with Why!

But when I trace upwards from F it isn't Y, but O. WHO! Of course! It's a whodunnit question! That's even better, because it's detective puzzling! And the next letter is P, which I know stands for W. And then A is A and J is S. And so far I have WHO WAS! And I'm so desperate to find out who was what that I speed through the Cipher, not even stopping to read what I've written. And I've only got two more letters to go when an old man taps me on the shoulder and says, "Excuse me, young lady, but..."

"I'm waiting for my mum," I answer back. "She won't be long. She forgot Dad's socks and they really need washing."

"Oh," says the man. "It's just that ... was that your dog outside...?"

"Wanda," I tell him. And I look up to give her a wave, but Wanda Wellingtons has gone!

I jump to my feet and the old man says, "A young lad untied her."

"Untied her!" I squeal. "What lad?"

"One of those from the park," says the man. "He's always hanging about."

"Otis!" I exclaim. And I dart outside, but Wanda has vanished, even her lead!

I race up and down, calling her name and walk around the back of the butcher's to see if someone might be hiding her there. I look behind the bins. I look IN the bins. I even look inside the butcher's shop in case she managed to escape from whoever took her and squeezed her way in. But she's not there either. No one is there. Just empty trays where sausages sat. I shout loudly and scour every inch of the shopping parade, but there's not a trace of her anywhere. I look up into a conker tree because if it was Otis who took her, he's very good at climbing trees. But all the conkers are long gone and most of the leaves have dropped off and it's almost bare and is not hiding Wanda. And then I think Wanda is clever and could outwit Otis (who's probably not as bright as a slug) and once she'd outwitted him she'd run home. And with this in my mind I run home too and cross my fingers my hunch is right. My heart's in my stomach as I rush through the door.

"Is Wanda here?" I panic.

"Isn't she with you?" asks Mum.

"No," I splutter. "And if she isn't here then she must still be stolen!"

"Stolen?!" laughs Dad. "Wouldn't you have noticed if Wanda had been stolen?"

"No," I tell him. "I was being distracted." And I stare at my feet in my slobbery clogs and mumble, "I was trying to crack the Chocolate Cipher and now Wanda's gone and she's the best dog ever!" And I explain about the launderette and the old man and a boy untying Wanda and how I looked for her everywhere. "It was probably, definitely Otis," I tell them, "and I hoped she might have escaped from him and run back home."

"Goodness," says Dad. "Why do you think it was Otis who took her?"

"The man said it was a lad from the park."

"But there are lots of lads in the park, Minnie. We can't just accuse Otis."

"But…" But I cannot tell Dad about the other day or he won't let me go to the park again.

"We'd better take a look around Hill Tops," he suggests. "We'll go on my motorbike. You come with me, Minnie, and Mum can stay here in case Wanda comes back."

"OK," I nod.

And he hands me my helmet and Mum gives me a hug and says, "There are lots of Jack Russells in Hill Tops, Minnie. Somebody probably thought she was theirs."

"But no other dog looks like Wanda," I sob. "And if she's been stolen we might NEVER find her."

"We will," says Mum and I chase after Dad with my lucky PARMA VIOLETS.

Dad and I search everywhere – up and down Arthurs Way, past the shops, around the park, past the school, behind the church, and all the roads that join them together. But Wanda isn't anywhere. We go round again to double-check and round again to triple-check but by now it's starting to get dark and Dad says we have to give up and he'll look again tomorrow.

"But I don't want to give up!" I protest. "Can't we try for five more minutes?"

"Of course," says Dad, and for one last time we go back to the butcher's.

"Where IS she?" I wail, as my tears drip on the empty pavement.

"Don't worry, Minnie. I expect someone's found her and our telephone number's on a disc on her collar, so I'm sure they'll give us a call. In fact they might be phoning right now."

But adults always say these things and when we get home no one has phoned and I'm so upset that I can't eat any of Mum's tea which is potato and garlic soup. I cross my fingers that someone will ring, but for once the flat is spookily silent. Even Spike has stopped screaming. And I know I wished for peace and quiet, but now I have it I don't want it. All I want is Wanda.

## TUESDAY DAY

### Where's Wanda?

I don't want to go to Frankie's today. I don't want to go anywhere, and when Gran comes to collect Spike she says, "Why don't I stay here and look after you, too?"

"Yes, please," I sob.

"Are you sure?" asks Mum.

"Sure," I mumble, and she rings Fabio to tell him the news and then she and Dad give me a hug, which makes me feel worse, because it's all my fault.

They leave for work and promise to phone the vets and the police station and I pace the corridor outside the flat, gazing over the balcony in the hope of spotting Wanda. But Wanda isn't there.

"What about knocking on a few doors?" suggests Gran. "Someone might have seen her."

"OK," I whimper, and Gran and Spike come with me and we start at Block A with Uncle Jeff's.

But he's not back from his milk round yet so we move along and when we get to Abhi's I cry, "I've lost Wanda. I don't suppose you've seen her, have you?"

"Sorry," says Abhi, "but I'll look for her when I go to the park."

"Thanks," I sniffle, and join Gran at Mrs Samson's. Mrs Samson says her rheumatism is playing up and she hasn't been anywhere to spot a dog unless Wanda jumped on her balcony in the middle of last night. She hobbles off to check, but comes back shaking her head.

Jasen answers at Flat 56 and he's non-stop sneezing, but says he'll text his dad and ask him to put a notice in his shop window.

At Flat 48 Mrs Bottomley says she's very sorry to hear the news, especially as Wanda is such a nice dog. "Not like some of the other dogs," she grumbles. "They're too big to be kept in flats. No wonder that Tyson keeps trying to escape. The poor dog needs a garden and—"

"How's Trevor?" I ask, interrupting. Mrs Bottomley is a non-stop natterer.

"A little better, thank you, Minnie. Not so hot, but he still can't swallow." And she pauses for breath.

"And he's so upset he missed his school trip. I'm afraid he loves chocolate more than he loves me!" And she laughs and says, "I'll tell him you called. He'll—"

"Thanks," I interrupt again. "Sorry, Mrs Bottomley, I have to go."

"Of course," she smiles.

Gran squeezes my hand as we shuffle back and forth between more doors but nobody's seen Wanda.

"Let's try Uncle Jeff's again," I suggest. "I know he'll help." And we climb in the lift and go back down to the ground floor, but there's still no answer.

"That's odd," says Gran. "He's usually back from work by now."

"Perhaps he's asleep," I tell her. "He must be tired after taking Dot to France."

"Maybe," says Gran. "Let's check Block B."

"All right," I sigh.

And we go back outside, through the garden and into an identical block of flats that have different people living inside them. And now I know how a tortoise feels because we seem to move so slowly. Everybody wants to chat and tell us stories about their own pets and invite us in for drinks and biscuits and they all smile and say, "Don't worry, Minnie, Wanda will come back very soon." And I try to smile back but it's grimacingly hard because I'm truthfully close to tears. I bite my lip so as not to cry and we keep knocking on all the doors, but every answer is always the same, No, No, No. Absolutely no one has seen Wanda. Tiffany and Otis's flat is next and I can't face seeing them, but as Otis is my top suspect I know I have to knock.

I send Gran up to the next floor and then sneak to their door and press my ear to the letter box. I am trying to hear Wanda barking, but it's trickily hard because Tiff's flat's even noisier than mine. I am just trying to decide what sounds are coming from the TV and what are real when Tiffany opens the door! We're both surprised to see each other but Tiff beams and says, "Hi, Minnie. You read my message! Come in!"

"Sorry, Tiff," I splutter. "I can't stay. I've lost Wanda. Someone untied her from outside Mr Bottomley's shop. I don't suppose you've seen her, have you?" And with every word I try to look past her and into her hall, but I can't see Wanda anywhere.

"No!" says Tiff. "Poor Wanda! Tyson got lost too. Do you remember when you..." And then she stops and says, "Shall I help you look for her?"

And she seems genuinely upset and I don't think she's lying, but I still don't want to play with her so I mumble, "No thanks, Tiff. I think I need to be on my own."

"Oh," says Tiff. "But I got you a pen..." And she looks down-in-the-dumps and wanders back inside her flat. She leaves the door open so I presume she's going to be coming back and I'm just wondering if I should make a run for it when she returns with a paper bag for me and a dog chew for Wanda. "Put the chew on your doorstep, Minnie, dogs love them. And if Wanda sniffs it she'll come straight home."

"Thanks," I smile.

And then Mrs Mead shouts, "Never mind chattering, Tiffany, come and put the kettle on."

"I'm coming," sighs Tiff.

And I can't help feeling a bit sorry for her. "You'd better go," I tell her. "Thanks for the chew."

"You're welcome," says Tiff. And Otis hollers and Tiff's face pales and she scurries back inside.

The lift in Block B has given up working and I find Gran struggling with Spike on the stairs. It's very bumpy, but the funny thing is that Spike seems to like it. He was crying earlier, but as soon as he bumps he forgets about his teeth and chuckles. I help Gran bounce him to the top floor and he's merrily gurgling and quite unaware that his lovely Wanda has disappeared. For a moment I wish that I was Spike, completely oblivious to this horrible moment, but then I hastily un-wish it because I don't want to be crying with toothache. And I make up my mind to stop wishing.

It's nearly taken the whole morning to call on everybody but there's still the top floor to cover. Gran goes back to my flat to start lunch and I knock on the last doors. I find myself guessing what everyone will say. "Sorry Minnie, we haven't seen her" or "We'll keep our eyes peeled". And with every flat I'm always right.

When I've been to them all I slump home and open Tiffany's paper bag and inside is a new pen. It smells of blackcurrants and dog chew, and I lay the chew by my front door and whisper, "Please, Wanda! Please come back."

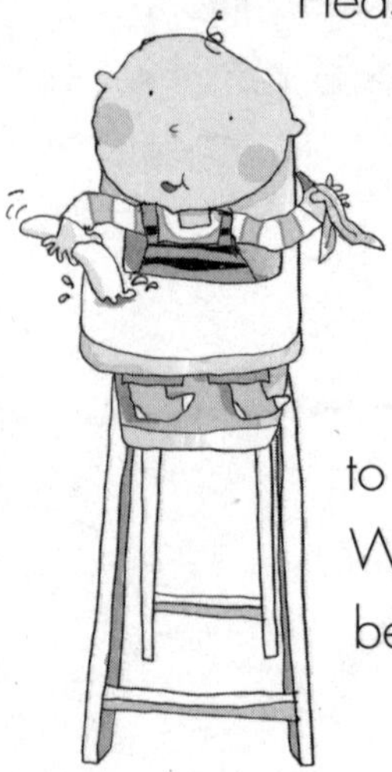

Gran serves me cheese on toast whilst Spike sits in his high chair pulverizing a banana.

"Now what do we do?" I ask.

"We stay put," says Gran. "We need to be here in case anyone finds Wanda. We've spread the word and people will be looking."

"But isn't that like giving up?" I sob.

"Of course not," says Gran. "And don't forget, Wanda has your number on her collar."

"Perhaps someone's already rung!" I exclaim. And I rush to the phone and the light is flashing, which means we have a message! "Someone's found her!" I squeal. And I press the button, but it's only Frankie and she hasn't found Wanda. She's just ringing to see if she's back.

"That's nice," says Gran. "Give her a call."

"No," I reply. "If I'm ringing out then people can't

ring in. If someone's found Wanda I need to be ready." But the light's still flashing and we have another message! I hold my breath and press the button and this time it's Mrs Bottomley. "Hello, Minnie," she says, "it's Trevor's mum here. You know he's poorly but he's such a good boy and…" And I have no desire to hear anything more about Trevor! I've spoken to his mum long enough this morning and I fast forward to the next message. But whoever it was hung up. But still the light flashes and we have six more messages. Five are blank and I'm about to give up when the next one speaks. But irritatingly it's Mrs Bottomley again. It's left about two hours after the first one and she seems to think that just because I asked about him I need a regular update on Trevor! But I don't care about her sweaty son! The only thing I care about is Wanda, and I delete the message before I hear it and burst into tears.

"I have to try and find her," I sob to Gran. "Maybe there'll be footprints I can follow, or a trail of dog hairs. There always are in films on TV. Would you mind waiting by the phone, Gran?"

"Only if you don't stay out long, Minnie. I don't want you going missing, too."

"I won't," I promise. And I tear down the steps and into the communal concrete garden where something grabs my eye. It's a drawing of Wanda stuck to a bin! Where on earth has that come from?! And more precisely, whose number is 726444? Spookily it rings a bell and I remember hearing it only recently. 726444. It's Trevor's number! I heard it on the answer machine. I'm totally puzzled. Why is there a drawing of Wanda on a bin with Trevor's phone number scribbled beneath it, as if Wanda was Trevor's dog? It's oddly peculiar and I take it down to show Gran later and then race through the garden past a telegraph pole, and yet another drawing! And as I skit through the alleys there are pictures of Wanda everywhere! Even as I head into Hill Tops, her pictures are Sellotaped to every lamp post and every shop window. There's a complete trail, right the way to Trevor's dad's shop!

What is Trevor Bottomley up to?

I sneak into BUBBLES Launderette to think. And what I think is that Trevor is another boy who hangs around in the park! And if it wasn't Otis who stole Wanda maybe it was him! But why would Trevor steal Wanda? And then I remember Otis picking on him after he'd saved me and Dot from Tyson. Otis must have sussed he was helping me so maybe he told Trevor to steal Wanda to prove he's his friend not mine! That's it! Trevor would never want to get caught helping girls!

But if he did steal Wanda, why would he put up posters of her? Unless ... now he feels guilty but can't hand her back without giving himself away! He'd be caught red-handed with dog hairs all over him! Mr and Mrs Bottomley would be really cross. But if he puts up posters with his phone number on them, he can claim someone has returned her to him. THEN he can hand her over to me and look like a hero. When really he's a low-down dog-thief!

It all fits and I storm into the butcher's and shout, "Where's Trevor?!"

"He's gone home, Minnie," says Mr Bottomley. "He's still not well and traipsing over Hill Tops was hard work. But he gave me a poster to put in the window and—"

"So I see!" I splutter.

And I tear it down and Mr Bottomley shouts, "Wait here, young lady! I have footage you know. Footage of your dog, caught on my camera and—"

"SO!" I shout back. "You shouldn't be spying. She wasn't breaking in. She was just trying to find some sausages." And I turn on my heels and run all the way home.

"Trevor's got Wanda!" I puff to Gran. And the phone is ringing but I'm in such a tizzy that we both ignore it.

"Thank goodness," says Gran. "Mrs Samson rang me and said he'd drawn some 'Lost' posters and stuck them up over Hill Tops. I'm so glad they worked."

"They didn't work," I tell her, laying a copy on the table. "That's probably him ringing now, but it's not what it seems. Trevor's pretending to be a hero when truthfully he dognapped Wanda! And now he feels guilty but he can't just own up and hand her over, so he's going to pretend that someone's phoned him and handed her in." And I go to grab the phone but it stops before I can pick it up and nobody leaves a message. "He's a dognapper, Gran, and he left a really big clue – he put HIS phone number across the bottom of the poster!"

"Ah, yes," says Gran. "Mrs Samson mentioned that. He's still poorly and not thinking straight. It was a silly mistake but nobody noticed till he'd printed them out."

"It's not a mistake at all," I tell her. "Don't trust him, Gran. Trevor's the very worst boy on the planet."

"Really, Minnie, I'm sure you've got it all wrong."

And the phone goes again and I snap it off the hook and if it's Trevor I'm turning him into sausages. But it isn't Trevor, it's Uncle Jeff and he splutters, "Thank goodness, you're back, Minnie. Where've you been? I've tried phoning you so many times, but all I get is your answer machine."

"Why didn't you leave a message?" I ask. "And

where have YOU been? We've lost Wanda and—"

"I hate talking on the phone," interrupts Uncle Jeff, "let alone talking to a beeping robot. Is your mum or dad there?"

"Only me, Spike and Gran."

"Put Gran on then."

I hand him to Gran, and Gran listens, and her face goes glum as she says, "I see. I'll ring Malcolm straight away." And she puts down the phone and says, "Well, dear, the good news is that Uncle Jeff has found Wanda. She wasn't at Trevor's she was—"

"Found Wanda!" I squeal. "Then why didn't he tell me?"

"Because the sad news is that she's—"

"Not DEAD!" I cry.

"No," says Gran. "But she is poorly. It looks as though she's been run over."

"RUN OVER!" I scream.

And Spike starts hollering, but this time I do not block my ears. I pick him up and hug him tight and whilst Gran phones Mum and Dad with the news we both can't stop sobbing.

# TUESDAY NIGHT

## Wishes

Mum comes home from work early and Dad goes to the vets. Uncle Jeff pops in to see how we are and says, "Hi, everyone. There are four dogs fighting over something on your doorstep."

"It's a dog chew," I tell him. "Tiffany gave it to me to lure Wanda back."

"That's thoughtful," says Uncle Jeff. "You've got some lovely friends, Minnie."

"Hmmmm," I mumble. "Tell me how you found Wanda."

"Well," says Uncle Jeff. "About 11.30 this morning I was driving home in my milk float when I saw Trevor's posters. They were all over Hill Tops and I recognized Wanda straight away. Then I spotted a tail behind a tree. I wouldn't usually have taken much notice, but with Trevor's posters clearly in my mind I went to take a look."

"Where was she?" asks Mum.

"Not far from the church. I think a car must have

knocked her over and she probably limped to the side of the road and found a good spot to stay safe."

"Was she yelping?" I worry.

"Only when I picked her up. Her back leg was hanging limp, so I wrapped her in my jacket and sat her next to me in the milk float whilst I rushed her to the vets. She knew it was her Uncle Jeff and that made her happy."

"So that's why you were late home!" I sigh. "Me and Gran came calling for you. I thought you might be asleep."

"Really?" says Uncle Jeff. "I kept ringing you but only got the answering machine. So I rang the number on the poster and it turned out to be Mrs Bottomley's. She told me Trevor had drawn the posters and I told her to thank him as they'd led me to Wanda and now she was with me at the vets. I asked her to tell you, but she must have forgotten."

"No, she didn't," I sigh. "She left two messages,

but I didn't listen to either. The first one must have been about Trevor putting the posters up and the second one was the message saying that you'd found her. But I didn't listen because I thought she was just going to harp on about Trevor."

"Oh," says Uncle Jeff. "Well, he's quite poorly, by all accounts, but when his mum told him that Wanda was missing he got very angry. He told her it was probably Otis Mead who untied her. He and Otis don't get on. Mrs Bottomley told me that last Thursday he came back from the park pretty shaken up. Otis had picked on him for some reason, but Trevor wouldn't say why."

"I know why," I mumble. "Trevor saved me and Dot when Otis set Tyson loose on Wanda. Dot was holding her and Tyson knocked them over and Trevor kicked his football so that Tyson would run after it and leave us alone..."

"Why would Otis set Tyson on Wanda?!" gasps Mum.

"Actually it might have been Dot he was after."

"Dot?!" asks Uncle Jeff. "What did Dot do to Otis?"

"She kept speaking to him in French, and he got

really cross and snatched her French dictionary. Tiff got it off him and took the blame, but lost a marble from our marble jar. Then we couldn't go to Cocoanuts and everyone got cross."

"But you DID go to Cocoanuts!" sighs Mum.

"Because Trevor won us another marble," I mutter.

"That Trevor keeps saving the day," says Uncle Jeff. "What a good lad he is. Been stuck in bed since Friday and got up specially to do those posters even though he still felt rotten."

And now I feel rotten too. Not only did I wish Trevor the mumps, but I've got him into trouble with Otis and Presley and suspected him of terrible things. When all the time he's been helping me. In the park. And with his posters. And I feel guiltily bad and am just about to hide in my room when the door opens and Dad walks in.

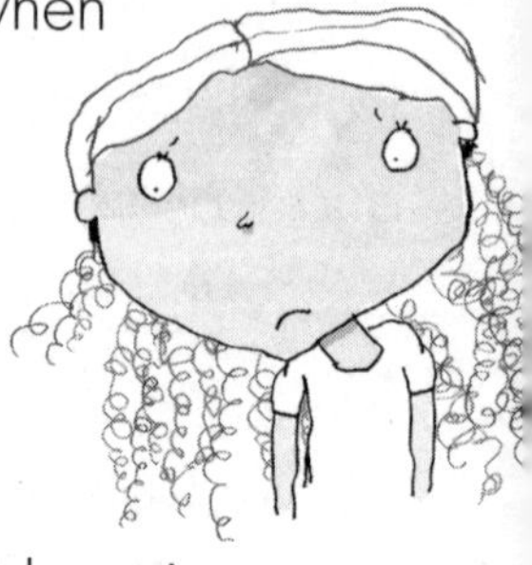

"Dad!" I squeal. "Where's Wanda?"

"She's still at the vets. But don't worry. She's going to be fine."

"Then why is she still at the vets?" I panic.

"She's resting," says Dad. "She's broken her leg and had to have an operation. It made her sleepy, but we can probably bring her home tomorrow."

"She's broken her leg! Oh, poor Wanda. How will she walk?"

"She's got a plaster cast," says Dad. "She'll be able to walk when she gets used to it, but I expect she'll lie quietly for a day or so."

Spike begins to howl and Mum sighs, "I wish you-know-who would lie quietly!"

"Don't say that," I splutter. "Take it back and don't make wishes. It's all my fault that Wanda's been run over. And that Trevor got the mumps. I wished for it and it came true."

"You wished for Wanda to be run over and Trevor to get the mumps?" gasps Mum.

"Not exactly," I tell her. "But it's all my fault." And I explain how I wished for Trevor to lose his voice so we wouldn't lose our trip to Cocoanuts, and how I'd made another wish to be left on my own so I had some peace to crack the Chocolate Cipher. "And both my wishes came true," I sob. "Trevor got the mumps and Wanda got dognapped and now I can do all the code-cracking I want. Only now I don't want to."

"Don't be silly," sighs Mum. "Of course it isn't your fault."

But in my heart I know it is, and silently I go to my room and hide deeply undercover. I don't want anyone to look at me and my mind spins as though it may never stop, and my bed feels so empty without Wanda. And I cannot sleep because I have to think of something good to somehow put things right.

# WEDNESDAY DAY

## Secrets

I decide to go to the Deli today and phone Frankie to check if it's OK. She sounds a bit upset and asks, "Are you sure you want to come?"

"Of course I do!" I tell her.

"OK, I'll see you later. I'm glad you've found Wanda."

"And me," I sigh. And I want to ask if she's feeling OK but she puts down the phone so I hang up. But immediately it rings back. She must be going to tell me something.

"Hello?" I answer. But it's not Frankie. It's Mrs Bottomley.

"Hello, Minnie. May I speak with one of your parents, please?"

She sounds very serious and must have found out I accused her son of dognapping Wanda! Nervously I pass the phone to Dad and Dad listens for a moment and then looks very cross and says, "I see, well thank you, Mrs Bottomley. I shall deal with this straight away." And he puts down the phone and calls Mum and I'm sure I'm about to be totally grounded, and there'll be no more Deli for the rest of the week, when he says, "Mr Bottomley has a security camera in his shop, Minnie, and he caught Wanda—"

"She wasn't doing any harm," I interrupt. "She was just looking for the sausages."

"He caught Wanda being untied by Otis!" says Dad.

"So it WAS him!" I cry.

"I'm afraid so," says Dad. "I'll call round and see him after I've dropped you at Frankie's."

"Don't!" I panic. "That'll just make things worse... Please don't go round. It'll cause more trouble and—"

"Don't worry," says Mum. "Dad knows what he's doing."

But I don't think he does. He doesn't know how horrid Otis is and now he'll never stop picking on me.

☆ ☆ ☆

When I get to the Deli, Frankie isn't as smiley as usual and is sitting at the counter chewing her hair.

"Are you OK?" I ask.

"I suppose so," she mumbles.

"You're not getting the mumps, are you?"

Frankie shakes her head but says nothing, so I tell her how Mr Bottomley has film footage of Otis untying Wanda. "Dad's going to tell him off, but I wish he wouldn't because now he'll be after me."

"You should keep away from the Meads, Minnie," she sulks. "Especially Tiff."

"She's not so bad," I tell her. "She has to help her mum a lot and her brothers are really horrible to her. I wouldn't want to be in her shoes."

"Really?" asks Frankie. "That's not what I've heard. I thought that's exactly where you wanted to be – in Tiffany's boots. You swapped them for your clogs. And don't say you didn't because Tiffany told me. She came to the Deli yesterday afternoon and told me you swapped secret messages. In Minnieglyphics! And I thought they were supposed to be our secret language?!"

"Sorry," I whisper. "I should have told you. I wanted to, but I thought you'd be cross and it was nothing really, and it didn't seem fair to upset you over nothing."

"Nothing?" cries Frankie. "I thought best friends didn't have secrets."

"They don't," I mumble. "It's just that Tiffany kind of forced her way in."

"She forced your feet into her boots?"

"No," I sigh. "But they were such nice boots and—"

"You've never asked to borrow my shoes. But perhaps they're not as nice as Tiff's."

"You've got amazing shoes. It's just these made me look like—"

"Tiffany!" blurts Frankie.

I shake my head. "Lavender," I whisper. "I thought if I could look a bit like her it might make me confident like her, too."

"Fibber!" says Frankie. "You borrowed the boots on Saturday and you didn't even know Lavender then."

"I didn't know her," I tell her, "but I saw her in Psychodelicious." And I spill the whole story of how

I couldn't think of what to buy and ended up copying Lavender with LOVE HEARTS and PARMA VIOLETS. "And then I wanted to write you a hieroglyphic message, but F was a snake and Gran suggested Minnieglyphics. I went to tell Dad and Tiffany heard me and asked to help, which Dad thought was a brilliant idea because it meant he could work on his motorbike."

"So you wrote secret messages in OUR secret language," snaps Frankie.

"Tiff wrote hers in Tiffanyglyphics," I mumble.

"Well I'm glad you had such fun," says Frankie. "Tiffany's obviously your new best friend."

"Of course she isn't."

"Then why didn't you phone me yesterday? I left you a message. I was desperate to hear any news of Wanda. And don't say you were too busy because you found time to talk to Tiffany. You actually went to her flat."

"But it's not how it sounds."

"Isn't it?" asks Frankie.

"I didn't just go to Tiffany's flat. I went to Abhi's and Jasen's and—"

"Fabiozo!" says Frankie. "That's why you had no

time for me! Well, I shouldn't worry. Lavender and I had a Fabaroony day. And as you say, she's so cool and—"

And she's obviously not going to listen to me so I interrupt her with, "I need to tell you something, Frankie. Something about Lavender. You said best friends shouldn't keep secrets, and I've been keeping this one for what seems like for ever. I couldn't tell you on Monday because I didn't want to spoil your birthday, but ... Lavender is two-timing Nero."

Frankie laughs.

"I saw her," I protest. "She was out on a date with— "

"With who?" snaps Frankie. "Trevor Bottomley!"

I shake my head. "I don't know if I should say. It's not his fault. Just like it isn't Nero's. But I saw them together, really I did. They were at the History Museum on Sunday."

"How come you're telling me this NOW?" shouts Frankie. "I seem to remember we were talking about YOU. You two-timing me with Tiff. And now you're twisting it and suddenly Lavender's been two-timing Nero!"

"You have to believe me. I saw them together.

Gran was with me. You can ask her. And there's even more proof. She'd already tried a Chocolate Gold Pyramid when I gave you yours on Monday. How did she manage that if someone from Class Chickenpox didn't give it to her? They're a brand-new sweet. You can't buy them in Psychodelicious."

"Who was it then?" snaps Frankie. "Who was she with at the History Museum?"

But before I can nervously give Abhi away Nero bounces in and says, "Hi, Minnie. Glad to hear you've found Wanda."

"Thanks," I tell him.

"Lavender won't be in today. She's busy doing secret things."

"Who with?" demands Frankie.

"It's a secret," laughs Nero.

Frankie and I stare at each other, but the door chimes and we turn to see who the customer is and heart-stoppingly scarily … it's Otis Mead! He's on his skateboard and next to him are Presley and Tiff. Frankie panics and my knees go to jelly, but Nero just smiles and says, "Can I help you guys?"

"No, thanks," grunts Otis. "We're 'ere to see Piper."

Nero looks at me and I look at Frankie.

"It's private," says Otis.

Fabio walks over and says, "Is everything OK?"

"Yes, thank you," says Tiffany. "We just need to speak to Minnie."

Shakily I ask, "Would you like an ice cream? My treat."

"No, thanks," says Otis. "We're in an 'urry."

"Perhaps we should talk outside?" suggests Tiff.

"OK," I nod, and before I know it I'm outside the Deli with two of the scariest boys on the planet.

And I worry what Dad has said to them and wait for Otis to charge at me, or hit me over the head with his deck, but instead he says, "This is for Wanda. I thought it might 'elp while she can't walk." And he hands me his skateboard.

"I don't understand. I…"

"Your dad says Wanda's hurt her leg," explains Tiff. "I thought you could sit her on the skateboard and push her about like a dog on wheels." And I cannot believe I'm hearing this, but Tiff hasn't finished and says, "Otis is sorry, aren't you, Otis?"

Otis almost nods his head and Tiff continues with, "Otis didn't mean for Wanda to get hurt. He was just getting his own back. He got into trouble when Tyson escaped when you threw my boots over the balcony. He was gone all night and Dad went mad and we were all so worried that Tyson was hurt and…"

"I never knew. You should have told me."

"We were grounded," snorts Presley. "And besides, we don't snitch."

"I'm sorry," I mumble.

"Don't be," says Tiff, glancing up the road. "We'd better be going. Mum's waiting."

And before I can take it all in, Otis, Presley and Tiffany have gone, racing up the road to meet their mother. I turn back to the Deli wondering what on earth Dad must have said to them.

"What was that all about?!" blurts Frankie. "And what's with the skateboard?"

"They've lent it to Wanda while she can't walk."

"Otis did that?" laughs Nero. "But he's superglued to that deck."

"Minnie's his sister's best friend," sulks Frankie. "They're into sharing things. Do it all the time."

And I try to protest, and point out that she shared my Minnieglyphics with Lavender. But she walks away and the café fills up and we have to start preparing the lunches. Frankie is non-stop twirling her hair and we do not speak as we make up the pizzas. Thankfully we are kept busy, but by two o'clock, when we stop for a break, Frankie says, "I can't believe I've lost my best friend and Nero's girlfriend all in one day."

"But you haven't lost me," I tell her. "I'm still your best friend. That's if Lavender isn't."

"Of course she isn't," says Frankie. "She's too grown up."

"And confident and cool and not silly like me."

"Exactly," says Frankie.

"Sorry," I tell her. "I don't know how it happened. Tiff's lonely and whilst you were away she latched on to me. And I wish she had a friend, really I do, just as long as that friend isn't me. And I wish you'd seen Abhi with Lavender yourself and then you might believe me."

"Abhi?!" exclaims Frankie. "ABHI is Lavender's other boyfriend?!"

I realize my mistake and nod.

"Just wait till I see him!"

"But he probably doesn't know she's seeing Nero. Nero doesn't know she's seeing Abhi."

"What a mess," sighs Frankie. And she screws her eyes tight and bites her lip. Then she jumps up and squeals, "But I know just the thing to get our brains working to sort it all out!" And she races to the counter and grabs two tall glasses and says, "We forgot about our Knickerbocker Glories! How do you want yours?"

And I'm so pleased to see her smiling again and recite, "Double chocolate, marshmallows and strawberries."

"Me too!" laughs Frankie. "Sounds Fabaroony." And with chocolate sauce she doodles on mine and on hers, which is M and F in Minnieglyphics, and they're the best letters I have ever tasted! "Chocolate's so delicious," she says. "I wish I could enter that chocolate competition and win a year's supply of Chocolate Gold Pyramids."

"Why don't you?" I ask. "I'll give you the details. I've almost done the decoding bit. Now I just need to answer the question."

"What question?" asks Frankie.

"I'm not sure. I haven't deciphered it yet. I've been too busy worrying about Wanda."

"And you call yourself an undercover puzzler?!"

"I've been an undercover worrier. I couldn't concentrate on cracking codes."

"But now you can! Have you got the Cipher with you?"

"It's in my pocket." And I put it on the table and spread it flat.

alphabet = A B C D E F G H I J K L M N O P Q R S T U V W X Y Z
cipher = A M U L E T V W X Y Z B C D F G H I J K N O P Q R S

secret message = PWF PAJ HNEED UBEFGAKIA XD BFOE PXKW?
WHO WAS QUEEN CLEOPATRA IN LOVE WI

And for the first time I read WHO WAS QUEEN CLEOPATRA IN LOVE WI...?

"Who was Queen Cleopatra in love with?!" squeals Frankie.

"That's easy," says Nero, coming to join us. "It's a pretty crazy story though."

"Tell us!" orders Frankie. "It could win us lots of chocolates."

"Really?" laughs Nero. "Well it goes like this ... Cleopatra was madly in love, but not just with one guy. She had her eye on two!"

"Two?" squeals Frankie, staring at me. "Who told you this story?"

"Lavender," grins Nero. "She's really into Cleopatra."

*And acting like her*, I think! I'm desperate to share my thoughts with Frankie but Nero is saying,

"First of all Cleo was in love with Julius Caesar, but then he died and she got kinda lonely and met two new guys at the same time, Mark Anthony and Augustus. She couldn't decide which one to go for, but opted for Mark Anthony. Bad choice. She chose the wrong man!"

Frankie and I are in disbelief. Is Lavender with Abhi this very moment making up her mind between him and Nero?

"Why was Mark Anthony the wrong man?" asks Frankie.

"He lost to Augustus in a battle," says Nero. "And Cleopatra thought he'd died. He hadn't of course, but she was so upset that rumour had it she took her own life."

"And did she?" I gasp.

"According to gossipers. But the crazy thing is,

Mark Anthony wasn't dead! And Cleopatra wasn't dead either. What they thought had happened, hadn't."

"So it all ended happily ever after?" asks Frankie.

"Should have done," sighs Nero, "but the rumours got in the way again. When Mark Anthony heard Cleopatra was dead he fell on his sword to die with her."

"But she wasn't dead!" gasps Frankie.

"Exactly," nods Nero. "And Mark Anthony was still alive when he found out, but by then it was sadly all too late. He died from his wound."

"That's gross!" says Frankie.

"What happened to Cleopatra?" I ask.

"She was so upset that she killed herself with a poisonous asp."

"What's an asp?" gasps Frankie.

"A snake," I tell her.

"No wonder you don't like them," says Frankie.

"Hey, it wasn't the poor old snake's fault," says Nero. "It was down to a host of gossipy people who spread untrue rumours."

Frankie and I glare at each other and Fabio calls Nero back to the kitchen.

"It's as if he knows!" whispers Frankie.

"Perhaps we should tell him?" I whisper back.

"No way," says Frankie. "I don't want to be one of those rumour-spreading gossips."

"Nor me," I gulp.

And I feel sick to my stomach as I finish my Knickerbocker Glory, though I'm not sure it's the food. I have the answer to the Chocolate Cipher and I thought I'd be happy that I've solved the code, but peculiarly I'm not.

## WEDNESDAY NIGHT

### Tongue-tanglingly tricky tiebreakers

"What's with the skateboard?" asks Dad when he comes to collect me. "You're not going to skate home are you?"

"Otis brought it for Wanda," I tell him. "He thought she could ride on it because she's broken her leg."

"That's a good idea," says Dad. "I'm glad he saw sense."

"What did you say to him?"

"I threatened to tell his dad and the police if he didn't go to the Deli and apologize to you and admit what he'd done."

"I thought he was coming to bully me or hit me over the head."

"I don't think he'd dare," says Dad. "Mr Mead is a tough man. A bit like me!" And he breaks into a smile and revs the engine of his motorbike and we roar all the way home.

"By the way," he grins as he opens the door, "a certain young lady is waiting to see you..."

"Wanda!" I squeal. "You're home!" And I give her a hug and she is non-stop swishing and wagging her tail. I look at her leg in a plaster cast and say, "I hope it doesn't hurt. But don't worry about not walking because Otis bought you this."

And I lift her on to

Otis's skateboard and

push her

into the kitchen.

Wanda barks and gets very excited, and I trundle her back and into the hall, and then to the table for tea. She slots in under my chair as I try to swallow beetroot soup and a pudding that's even sharper than lemons. My eyes water as I tell Mum and Dad about my day and how I've almost solved the code.

"Now I just have to think of a tiebreaker," I tell them. "Why I should be the winner, in no more than 25 words."

"That's easy!" says Dad. "Just tell them you're nuts about Cocoanuts chocolates!"

"But EVERYONE will say that," I tell him. "It has to be special to get me noticed."

"Draw a picture to go with it," says Mum.

"But they just want words!"

And they're obviously not going to be any help so I push Wanda into my room. But my room is not at all as I left it!

"What's happened?" I shout. "Why is my mattress on the floor?"

Dad sticks his head around my door and grins, "I thought you'd be sad if you couldn't sleep with Wanda. She can't jump up so we've brought you down."

"That's brilliant, Dad! You're a genius."

And then Spike starts crying and Mum calls for Dad to comfort him. "I always get the good jobs," he smiles.

"He likes bumping up and down steps," I tell him. "It stops him crying. At least it did for me and Gran."

"Really?" asks Dad.

And he disappears to give it a try as I nestle Wanda on to my mattress. Then I go to my dressing table for my goody bag of Pyramids, and there are five left so I take two and go back to my bed and unwrap them.

"We deserve these," I whisper to Wanda. "It's a very special day. You're back and Frankie is my friend again. AND I've cracked the Cipher." And I give her her own Chocolate Pyramid and she swallows it whole as if she's in doggy heaven and I think about a tiebreaker.

It's not at all easy and now I know why they're called tiebreakers – they tie your brain in a zillion knots and after squillions of scribblings you cannot get a break and find an answer. I try, "I SHOULD WIN A YEAR'S SUPPLY OF CHOCOLATE GOLD PYRAMIDS: because I think they're lip-smackingingly, finger-lickingly mind-bogglingly dreamy", but it's too tongue-tanglingly tricky to read. So I try something simpler with, "because I think your chocolates are Fabaroony!" But Frankie will probably have written this, so I decide to creep, just a little, and doodle, "... Cocoanuts chocolates are better than the real Willy Wonka could make. Hooray for Brian and Cleopatra!" And I read it to Wanda, but Wanda ignores me, so it can't be good and it's nibble-my-fingernails frustratingly annoying because I'm so near and yet so far, and I'm not even sure how long I have before I need to email the answer.

I open my treasure box for the list of rules and, as I remove the sheet of gold paper, there beneath it is a not-so-glitzy brown envelope saying HALF-TERM HOMEWORK. I'd completely forgotten all about it and tear it open and lay it on my pillow and it's a

*Hieroglyphic* wordsearch puzzle!

I stare at…

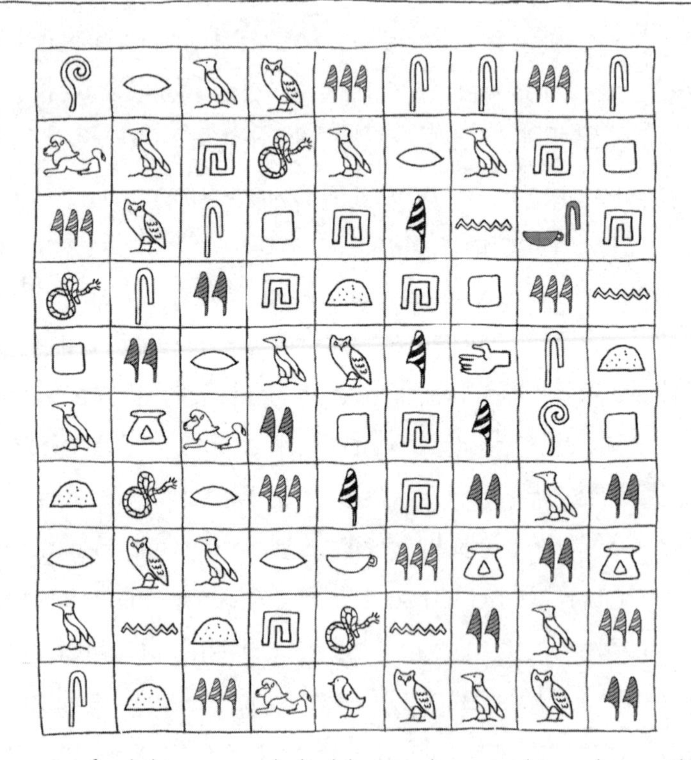

Can you find these words hidden in the wordsearch puzzle?

CLEOPATRA PYRAMIDS AMULETS EGYPT NEPHTHYS PHARAOH SPHINX RAMESSES HIERO GLYPHIC MARK ANTHONY RA

Good luck Chickenpoxers. Once you have found them all, select one of the subjects and see what you can find out about it.

Have a fun holiday, Mr Impey.

And it's such cool homework and I love wordsearch puzzles almost as much as I love chocolate! I show it to Wanda and start to translate the list of words I must find and so far I have doodled

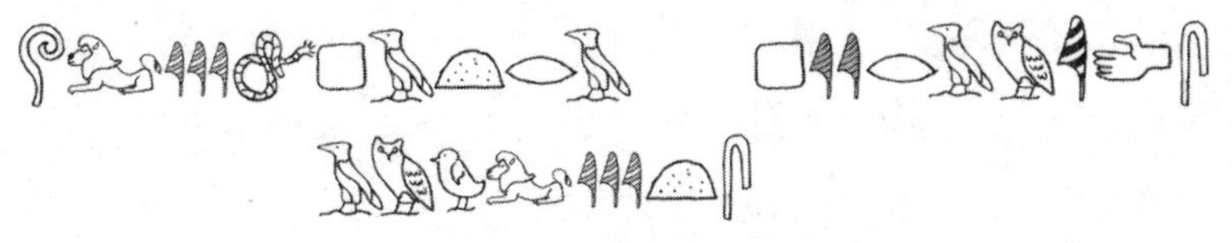

which hopefully spell CLEOPATRA, PYRAMIDS and AMULETS.

Mum comes in to check if Wanda's OK, but she shouldn't have worried because she's cocoaly happy. But I can't tell Mum this so I explain what we're doing and she looks at the homework and says, "It might be easier to turn the puzzle into English, Minnie. It'd be a lot quicker to spot the words."

And this is actually quite a brainiac idea and I wonder if perhaps she's cool after all. "Are you and Dad designers?" I ask.

"What makes you say that?" laughs Mum.

"Nero said you were."

"Well that's nice. At least someone appreciates what we do. Unlike some young monkey I could mention." And she goes off to attend to Spike who is back from his bouncing and sobbing miserably.

Wanda pricks her ears and tunes in to his howls and then buries her head in her paws. "Think about something else," I tell her. And I look at my list and the last word is Ra and I distract her with, "Ra was an ancient Egyptian Sun God. He bobbed about the skies of the Netherworld in a little boat at night."

Wanda likes this and barks, "Ra!"

And whilst she is happy I get on with my puzzle and it takes me for ever but finally I decipher...

| | | | | | | | | |
|---|---|---|---|---|---|---|---|---|
| C | R | A | M | E | S | S | E | S |
| L | A | H | O | A | R | A | H | P |
| E | M | S | P | H | I | N | X | H |
| O | S | Y | H | T | H | P | E | N |
| P | Y | R | A | M | I | D | S | T |
| A | G | L | Y | P | H | I | C | P |
| T | O | R | E | I | H | Y | A | Y |
| R | M | A | R | K | E | G | Y | G |
| A | N | T | H | O | N | Y | A | E |
| S | T | E | L | U | M | A | M | Y |

Now all I need to do is to search for the words and I'm just looking for Cleopatra when Dad comes in to turn off my light.

"My motorbike's gone to bed,too," he smiles.

"To BED?" I laugh.

"Yes," he grins. "It was too tired to go for a spin. TWO TYRED!" And he spells it out which makes it worse and adds, "Have you thought of a tiebreaker, Minnie?"

"Not yet," I tell him. "But don't panic, I've checked the rules and I've still got until noon tomorrow!"

"Don't be choco-LATE!" he smiles. "And by the way, I think you should thank Trevor for helping us find Wanda."

"I will," I promise.

"Don't forget. That's two things you need to remember! The tiebreaker and Trevor. It should be easy. They're the two T's!"

And he has no idea that I call Trevor and Tiffany the two T's, but I push them both to the back of my mind as he turns off my light.

Once he has gone I flick on my alien pen and get back to my homework, and there are thirteen missing words to find and some are easy and some are stubbornly, impossibly tricky and I cannot find EGYPT anywhere. I go back and forth and from corner to corner diagonally, but I still cannot see it. But it might be because it is yawningly late and my eyes keep shutting, and if I'm going to get up for work tomorrow then I'd better get some sleep.

I put the wordsearch on the floor and whisper, "Night-night, Wanda. It's so good to have you back."

"Ra," woofs Wanda.

And like Sun Goddesses we fall asleep.

# THURSDAY DAY

## Two-timing Cleopatra

It is spookily peculiar, but the minute I wake up I stare at the wordsearch and immediately find EGYPT. It's probably because I've been dreaming about it and me and Frankie were dressed in togas and feasting on Egyptian pyramid-shaped pizzas. But when I get to the Deli, Frankie's just in her jeans and T-shirt, nibbling on a croissant.

As I join her she whispers, "Don't look now, but here comes the two-timing Cleopatra. Let's hide and see what she does."

We duck behind the counter and I can just see Lavender's pointy boots walking over to Nero. We listen as she says, "There's something I really have to tell you, Nero."

And we glare at each other and know just the something she has to tell.

"She's going to confess!" whispers Frankie. "SHE must know that WE know, and she has to come clean."

And my heart goes out to poor Nero, and although I want Lavender to own up I clutch my VIOLETS and wish really hard that she'll say something nice.

"It's kind of a surprise," she whispers.

And me and Frankie prick up our ears and wait for the rest. But surprisingly Nero gushes, "Cool present! And it's not even my birthday."

"It's a sorry-she's-been-cheating-on-him present!" whispers Frankie.

But the surprise is that it isn't!

"It's an I-really-missed-you-whilst-you-were-in-Italy present," says Lavender. "I didn't know how to tell you, so I thought I'd make you this." And our heads bob up to see what it is and Lavender whispers, "I was so lonely that I even went to the museum with my cousin!"

And quietly her words sink in and Frankie turns and glowers at me and totally forgets she's hiding. "You went to the History Museum with your COUSIN?!" she squeals.

Lavender and Nero jump. They had no idea we were so close and Nero blushes, but Lavender sighs, "Sad, I know, but he was trying to find out about Egyptian things and I'm so into Cleopatra."

"Hmmmm," humphs Frankie, still glowering at me.

And I cannot believe that Abhi Talwar is Lavender's cousin! I met one of his cousins ages ago but she was a geek called Rita.

Nero unwraps his present and it's a purple drum kit made out of cardboard, and inside are three Chocolate Gold Pyramids.

"Cool," says Nero.

"I got the Pyramids from Abhi," she says, "as a present for taking him to the History Museum. But I copied the whole idea from Minnie. I loved the casket she made so much and..."

And I cannot believe she copied ME! But I can't bear to listen any longer, and I don't want to talk so I shuffle off to the kitchen and pretend I've got a sore throat and that maybe I'm getting the mumps like Trevor.

"Serves you right!" snaps Frankie. "You're a rumour-spreading gossiper!"

And my insides twist together and all of me hurts but is peculiarly numb at the same time. "I'm sorry," I mumble. But Frankie ignores me and we don't speak until morning break when Fabio serves us four slices of died-and-gone-to-heaven chocolate cake. Nero tucks in, but Frankie says she isn't hungry and Lavender resists and asks if she can have an orange juice instead.

"Lavender's really into wholefoods," boasts Frankie, making out she knows everything about her.

"It's my mum's fault," sighs Lavender. "She's a yoga teacher and health nut!"

"Doesn't your mum do yoga, Minnie?" asks Nero.

I nod my head and Lavender says, "That's so cool. A designer, a mural artist and a yogi! What's the name of her teacher, Minnie?"

"Mina," I mumble.

"Never!" laughs Lavender. "That's my mum!"

"Really?!" I gulp. "No-sugar Mina?!"

"That's the one!" laughs Lavender.

"But don't you mind not eating sugar?"

"Not really. In fact I quite like it. It's made my skin and hair really nice."

And I finger my own hair and the spot that is bubbling up on my chin. This week I've eaten so much chocolate! Chocolate pyramids, chocolate doughnut, chocolate sphinx, hot chocolates, chocolate ice cream Knickerbocker Glories, not to mention Brian Willy Wonka's zingy-chilli, fruity raspberry, spicy orange and breath-fresh peppermint!

Frankie starts pretending that she's really into wholefoods, too, and gets up to fetch a juice. I know she is fibbing and can't tell a walnut from Trevor's brain, but I bite my tongue and after a few minutes Nero nudges me and says, "Are you OK, Minnie? You seem kinda quiet."

"At least she's not spreading rumours," snaps Frankie.

"I can't imagine Minnie doing that!" laughs Lavender.

"Oh, she does," says Frankie. "Tell her, Minnie. Tell Lavender what you told me."

Lavender and Nero stare at me and I close my eyes so I don't have to see them and whisper, "I told Frankie I thought Lavender was two-timing Nero."

"Two-timing?!" laughs Lavender. "How did I manage that?"

"And who with?" gasps Nero.

"Abhi," I mumble.

"ABHI?" laughs Lavender. "But he's my cousin!"

"I've only met one of his cousins and she's called Rita."

"But I AM Rita!" laughs Lavender. "Only Nero calls me Lavender as I'm crazy about everything purple! I thought you recognized me because you said hello in Psychodelicious and the History Museum."

"You're Rita?" gasp me and Frankie together.

"Of course I am! Don't you recognize me? I know I'm two years older than you, but I did go to Hill Tops school."

"Only in Year Six though," says Nero.

"And Rita Talwar had a long plait," says Frankie, "and was geeky and plump and … and nothing like YOU."

"Thank goodness!" laughs Lavender. "What a sight I was. It all changed with Mum's new cooking. But you did the right thing, Minnie. I hope someone would tell me, if they saw Nero with another girl!"

Nero pretends to be panic stricken, but offers me a reward of a Chocolate Gold Pyramid.

I shake my head but Frankie grabs one and says, "Minnie always knows what to do. That's why she's my best friend. At least I hope she is. I'm sorry I called you a rumour-spreader, Minnie. You're not really."

"Of course I'm your friend," I sigh. And I give her a hug as she unwraps Nero's chocolate.

"I love these yummy Pyramids," she grins. "Did you think of a tiebreaker, Minnie?"

"Not yet," I tell her, suddenly remembering Dad's instructions.

"Why ever not? You need to win the competition!"

"I couldn't think of anything to say."

"Nor me," sighs Frankie, "but I sent it off anyway." And she looks at the clock behind the counter and grins, "You still have fifteen minutes. Go to Dad's office and think of something. NOW!"

"But I can't decide what to say," I tell her. "I can NEVER decide on anything. Not like Lavender."

"Like me?!" laughs Lavender. "I can NEVER decide on anything, either! That's why I always opt for purple!"

"Really?" I ask.

"Really," sighs Nero.

And suddenly I feel much better and race off to Fabio's office.

I need to answer the question and say who Cleopatra was in love with and decide to recount the whole story, just in case it's a trick question. And whilst I'm thinking up a tiebreaker I type an apology for my answer being last minute, and explain that Spike's teething and it makes him noisy and it's been trickily hard to think.

But it's even harder to think why I should win a year's supply of chocolate when I'm kind of going off it. I've eaten so much I can barely face another mouthful and I twiddle my thumbs till … my brain fizzes and suddenly I have my tiebreaker! Frantically I begin to type and the computer clock says 11.52 and my fingers whizz across the keyboard, but they cannot keep up with my brain. At 11.58 I check what I've written and with a minute to spare I hit  send.

"Have you done it?" asks Frankie, when I get back to the counter.

"I've done it!" I nod.

"So, what did you put for your tie-breaker?"

"It's a secret," I giggle.

"But I thought best friends didn't have secrets!"

"I'll tell you if I win!" I promise.

"OK," sighs Frankie. "But guess what? Lavender's had a Fabaroony idea and she mentioned it to Dad and Dad said YES!"

"What sort of an idea?" I ask.

"A chocolaty Egyptian idea," grins Lavender. "We were all so jealous that we didn't go to Cocoanuts, so I thought maybe we could bring Cocoanuts to us!"

"We're going to transform the Deli!" laughs Frankie.

"Into a chocolate factory?" I gasp.

"Not quite," says Fabio. "But I thought we could have an Egyptian day!"

"That's brilliant!" I tell him.

"And it's tomorrow," giggles Frankie, "so we have to think up a menu."

"That's easy!" I tell her. "Pyramid Pizzas! They were in my dream."

"Fantastico!" beams Fabio. "But what about pudding?"

"I know that too! Pyramis cake. It's shaped like a pyramid and Gran's got the recipe on a tea towel."

"Bravo!" claps Fabio. "That's the menu sorted and Lavender has dealt with the rest."

"She has?" asks Frankie.

"Sure," says Fabio. "I knew it would take some careful planning so I gave her the day off to come up with ideas."

"What ideas?" I ask.

"Cocoanutty Egyptian ideas!" laughs Lavender. "We'll all wear togas and put sand on the floor and—"

"So that's what you were doing yesterday?" interrupts Frankie. "Thinking about togas and sand?"

"Why?" asks Lavender. "What did you think I might be doing?"

"Nothing," we giggle. "Nothing."

## FRIDAY

### Surprise! Surprise! Surprise!

The Deli looks amazing. Outside there's a blackboard announcing

Minelli's Deli EGYPTIAN EXTRAVAGANZA

and either side of the door are two cardboard palm trees! But inside it gets even better. The lights have been dimmed and gold fairy lights sparkle across every wall and each of the tables has a gold paper tablecloth and a chocolate-scented candle, making the whole Deli smell like Cocoanuts! There's sand on the floor and the menu on the blackboard behind the counter is decorated with hieroglyphics, and the packets and tins on all the shelves have been stacked to look like pyramids.

Frankie, Nero and Lavender are dressed in togas and Frankie says, "Quick, Minnie, we need to get you dressed before the customers come in!"

"It looks amazing!" I squeal as they bundle me into Fabio's office.

"I know," giggles Frankie, "and you're going to look amazing too!"

And she makes me a toga from a white sheet that authentically says 100% Egyptian cotton. Then Lavender paints black around our eyes and I'm just wondering if Fabio's dressing up when he comes jaunting in in a hairnet!

"That's not Egyptian!" laughs Frankie.

But I recognize him immediately. "He's Brian Willy Wonka Wilson! Or rather, Fabio Willy Wonka Minelli!"

Fabio grins and we all laugh, but the door chimes and we dive into the Deli to greet our first Egyptian customer. It's Mrs Elliott and she orders a Ra-ppuccino, which is a frothy coffee fit for the Sun God, Ra, and Nero pours it and I hold a triangle stencil over it whilst Frankie sprinkles chocolate powder. When I remove the stencil there's a chocolate pyramid floating on top! Mrs Elliott is very impressed and her moustache twitches as she takes a sip. Then the door chimes again. And again. And again. At half past eleven, Brainiac Jenny comes in with her mum. She's the cleverest girl in the whole of the universe and she says, "Did you win the competition, Minnie?"

"No one's phoned," I tell her.

"I was a runner-up and won a week's supply of Pyramids."

"Really?!" I exclaim. "That's good." And I'm glad she's won something. She deserves it after traipsing about Cocoanuts with Tiff.

"I've just been finishing my homework about Ramesses," she says.

"Who's Ramesses?!" asks Frankie. "And what homework?"

"Ramesses was a famous pharaoh," says Jenny.

"We got a wordsearch for homework," I explain. "And it's full of Egyptianish things and you have to find out about one of them. I think I'm going to do amulets."

"What will I do?" panics Frankie. "D'you think I could do amulets, too? You did buy me that scarab, Minnie."

"Or," suggests Lavender, who's come to join us, "you could do Nephthys! You love goddesses and I know she's on the list because I've been helping Abhi."

"I've got my kite!" squeals Frankie. "My Nephthys kite! And I found her hidden name on the tail and I could change it from Minnieglyphics to Fr—" and then she bites her tongue and splutters, "Have you eaten your prize, Jenny?"

"Not yet. I just got an email telling me I'm a runner-up. They're going to post me the Pyramids."

"Email?" asks Frankie. "Not a phone call?"

"They're only phoning the winner, I think."

"Then maybe we're runners-up, too!" screeches Frankie. "Did you check your emails, Minnie?"

"Not yet," I tell her.

"Let's do it now! Seven Pyramids are better than none." And we rush to Fabio's office and scan our emails, but there is absolutely zilch.

"Not even runners-up," I sigh.

"But," says Frankie, "if we're not runners-up we could still be winners! Or rather YOU could, you're the puzzler. And it's not the twelve o'clock deadline yet! But wait a minute, you're not at home, Minnie! They might have phoned and you're not there!"

"Gran's there," I tell her. "She promised to wait in, just in case."

"But she might have forgotten!"

"Not Gran. She's totally reliable and would never break a promise."

But the clock strikes twelve and Gran doesn't ring and it's now lunchtime and everybody wants pyramid pizzas. And we've given them Egyptian names and shout,

And everybody loves them and I forget all about the Chocolate Cipher until the door opens and who should rush in, but Gran and Spike! And she's flushed pink and it looks as though she might've been running. But why would Gran run, if not to tell me something important? Gran never runs! Perhaps I have won after all!

"Hello, dear," she puffs. "You forgot to take my tea towel with the Pyramis recipe on."

"Oh," I mumble.

"And?" says Frankie.

"Should there be something else?" pants Gran.

"Did Brian Willy Wonka ring?" I ask.

"Oh, I'm afraid not, dear. I stayed in. That's why I'm late with the recipe. Poor Fabio will be desperately waiting."

And I'd completely forgotten about the cake and I take the tea towel and Spike starts to cry and he's embarrassingly loud and Gran says, "Better dash. I think I've got some bumping to do."

And I try to smile, and open the door to help her out, but secretly my heart is down in my clogs.

Frankie disappears and then comes back grinning and says, "I know it's not as good as winning a year's supply of Pyramids, Minnie, but I made you this." And she hands me a messy glittery envelope.

I tear it open and inside is a handmade card and on the front is a doodle of someone and I think it's probably, definitely Cleopatra.

"Thanks!" I smile. "It's really good."

"It's Nephthys," she says, "but the important bit's inside."

And I flip the card open and it's head-to-toe filled with peculiar scribblings.

"It's a Frankieglyphics secret message!" laughs Frankie. "I invented them last night. And I nearly let slip in front of Jenny, but I don't want anyone to know about them. Not even Lavender. They're just OUR secret!"

And she hands me a sheet of silver paper and it's star-shaped with gold glitter around the edge.

"It looks even better than Cleopatra's pyramid-shaped Chocolate Cipher!" I tell her.

"Thanks," giggles Frankie. "I'll serve the customers and you get cracking."

"Now?" I ask.

"Now!" demands Frankie.

And I stare at the message but she's hopeless at codes and I haven't a clue what she has written.

"How are you doing?" she whispers.

"Quite good," I fib.

And I decipher the Frankieglyphics and read...

!REDNEVAL RO FFIT LLET TON DNA SDRAWKCAB SCIHPYLGEIKNARF DNA EINNIM LLEPS S'TEL

And it's odd that it starts with an exclamation mark. Unless … it's a backwards message! And if it is, it says…

LET'S SPELL MINNIE AND FRANKIEGLYPHICS BACKWARDS AND NOT TELL TIFF OR LAVENDER!

"Our own special language!" I squeal, finally solving it.

"I know!" grins Frankie. "A back-to-front language! We'll try it out later, but we'd better give Dad this Pyramis recipe!"

I rush it to him but Fabio says, "Sorry, Minnie, but there's no time. The customers need their puddings now."

"Oh," I sigh. "Then how about Egyptian ice creams?! We'll ask everyone their initials and doodle them in chocolate-sauce *hieroglyphics* on top."

"And I could arrange wafers to look like pyramids!" says Frankie.

"Fantastico!" agrees Fabio.

And the customers love them. Even if they're

bursting from too much pizza they make a space for an Egyptian ice cream and by three o'clock we've almost run out. But thankfully the Deli empties too.

Fabio comes out of the kitchen beaming, "Well done, you two. You've been such good salesgirls that we've sold out of pizzas!"

"Oh, no!" squeals Frankie. "What will we eat? I really wanted a pyramid pizza."

"Don't worry," laughs Fabio. "I've saved you one each." And the door chimes again and it's Abhi and Jasen, and Jasen is obviously feeling better and come for a pizza to celebrate. I worry that Fabio will

give them ours, but before I can mention it, Tallulah and Delilah, the twins, come in. And then Brainiac Jenny and Tiffany Me-Me, followed by Kevin Little, Daniel Jackman and half of Class Chickenpox!

"I hope none of you want pizzas," sighs Frankie. "I'm afraid we've sold out."

Everyone's face instantly drops until Fabio says, "Only teasing. Please take your seats. Nero, will you do the door?"

Nero grins and locks the door and flips the sign from OPEN to CLOSED.

"What's going on?" asks Frankie.

"SURPRISE!" shouts Lavender.

"Happy Belated Egyptian Birthday Party," says Nero.

"Party?!" laughs Frankie.

"Party!" beams Fabio. "Sorry it's late, but we couldn't have a party without your mum." And suddenly Violetta appears and she is wheeling a

trolley
piled
high
with
pyramid
pizzas.

"Mum!" cries Frankie. "When did you get back?!"

"This morning," chuckles Violetta. "But I've been a bit busy." And she gives Frankie a big hug and says, "Wait there," and goes back to the kitchen and returns with a tray of amulet biscuits and they look like scarabs and have currants for eyes. But she hasn't finished. One more trip and she comes back with the centrepiece, which is a wobbling sphinx jelly!

"Fabaroony!" cries Frankie.

And it totally is. But Violetta still hasn't finished. "Would anyone like a drink?" she asks. "We have Egyptian cocktails – Strawberry Sphinx or Sun God Ra-spberry!"

"Sun God!" I shout.

"Strawberry Sphinx!" cries Frankie.

And everybody places their orders and Fabio returns with even more pizzas. And the toppings look like hieroglyphics!

"I wonder who won the Chocolate Gold Pyramids?" asks Abhi.

"It wasn't you then?" I ask.

"I wish," he sighs.

And then the door tries to open and someone is banging on it to get in and it's Mrs Bottomley, red in the face. Nero gets up to open it and she says, "I was wondering if you might have a pizza left. Trevor's suddenly got his appetite back. He's only gone and won a year's supply of chocolate!"

Everybody's mouth drops open and Frankie says, "Trevor won the competition?!"

"He's so clever," says Mrs Bottomley.

And I'm not sure they're talking about the same Trevor. All of Class Chickenpox are speechless, but Tiffany can't keep quiet for long and whispers, "But he didn't even go to Cocoanuts!"

"Or have an entry form," mutters Frankie.

"Perhaps Mr Impey sent him one," I mumble, "to keep him occupied whilst he was poorly."

Frankie looks at me and pulls a face and Kevin says, "At least someone from our class won it."

"And he did win the last marble," offers Jenny. "We wouldn't have gone to Cocoanuts without him."

"And he helped Minnie find Wanda," reminds Tiffany.

And we all try to smile and Frankie sighs as we think why Trevor deserves to win.

"And he saved Dot and Wanda from Tyson," adds Nero.

"Enough!" cheers Fabio. "He's fantastico! And such an occasion warrants a Cleopatra Special!" And we all fall silent again as he goes to the kitchen and returns with a ginormous flat box. He bows and hands it to Trevor's mum.

"Goodness!" flushes Mrs Bottomley. "Trevor will be pleased."

And she trots off and Frankie bolts the door and panics, "Just in case Trevor comes back to say thank you! I can barely believe it. I was so sure you'd win, Minnie."

"Don't worry," I sigh. "I've kind of gone off chocolate anyway."

"I hope you haven't gone off pizzas!" cries Fabio.

"No way!" I tell him. "Especially pyramid-shaped pizzas!"

"Buono!" sighs Fabio.

And everyone tucks in and it's a truly scrumptious Egyptian feast. So good that slowly we all forget about Trevor and start on the curranty amulet biscuits and wobbly sphinx jelly.

And when we have finished, Fabio gets up and dims the fairy lights and Violetta comes in with a sparkling cake. A sparkling, pyramid, Pyramis cake! And three gold sparklers are sticking out the top and fizzing like my stomach.

"You made it!" shouts Frankie.

"By the skin of our teeth!" grins Violetta.

And it's totally delicious and even though we're all full we gobble it all up.

Abhi sighs, "I feel like an ancient Egyptian mummy – completely stuffed!"

And we all laugh and a horn beeps and we look outside and it's Dad on his motorbike … with Wanda sitting in a box on the back! Everyone fusses her and all the other parents arrive and it's time to go home.

Soon the only ones left are me and Frankie. "It's been such a good day," I smile.

"Mmmmm," says Frankie. "Especially for Trevor!"

"And me," I tell her. "And you!" And I pull on my crash helmet and clamber on to the bike with Wanda.

Dad starts the engine and says, "Oh, by the way a parcel came for you, Minnie. Maybe you won that chocolate competition!"

"Maybe!" I smile.

"Minnie?!" squeals Frankie. "Minnie Piper! You DID win it, didn't you! Trevor couldn't have. Like Tiffany said, he didn't even go to Cocoanuts. Plus he can't puzzle to save his life. Someone must have won those chocolates for him. And I bet that person was—"

"GO!" I shout to Dad. And Dad revs the engine and we zoom off and Frankie is chasing us and Dad laughs and says, "What was that all about?"

"Tell you later," I grin. And then me and Wanda hold tight and whizz all the way home.

The flat is even noisier than usual. Mum has the music on and is dancing with a screaming Spike in her arms. "He's finally cut his tooth!" shouts Mum. "The only trouble is he's got another two on the way."

"That's my boy!" hollers Dad.

And I give Spike a kiss and my ears nearly burst as he howls into them, and Wanda seems to think we're playing a game of who can be loudest and begins to bark like Tyson.

"I think I'll go to my room," I shout.

"Good idea!" Dad hollers back. "Look on your mattress!"

And with all the pandemonium I nearly forgot about my parcel! But there on my bed is a bulging gold envelope! I rip it open and it's from Brian and Cleopatra.

And mind-bogglingly brilliantly it says…

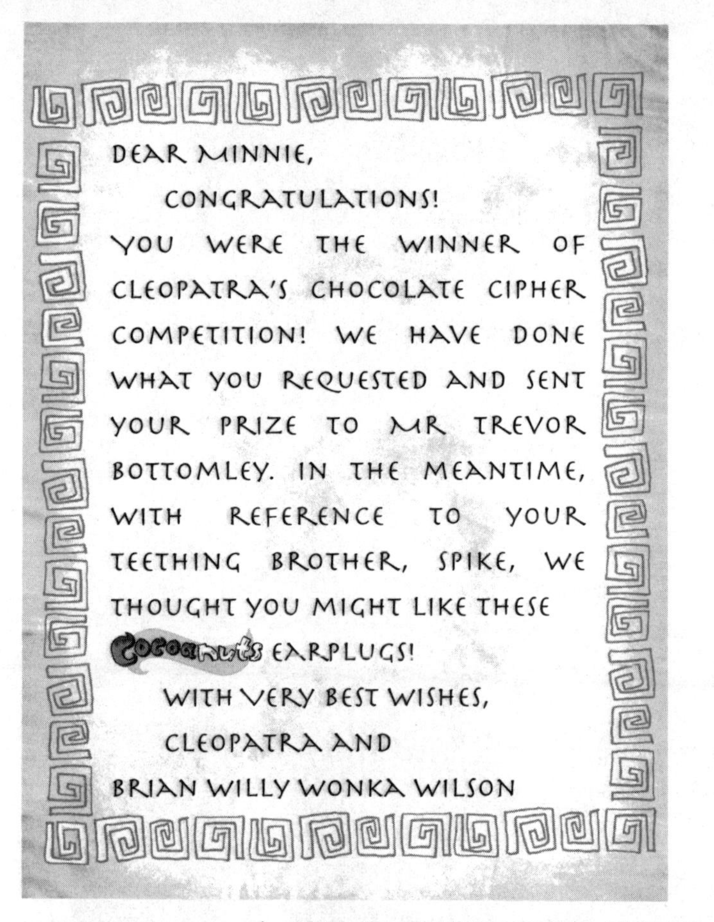

DEAR MINNIE,

CONGRATULATIONS!

YOU WERE THE WINNER OF CLEOPATRA'S CHOCOLATE CIPHER COMPETITION! WE HAVE DONE WHAT YOU REQUESTED AND SENT YOUR PRIZE TO MR TREVOR BOTTOMLEY. IN THE MEANTIME, WITH REFERENCE TO YOUR TEETHING BROTHER, SPIKE, WE THOUGHT YOU MIGHT LIKE THESE Cocoanuts EARPLUGS!

WITH VERY BEST WISHES,

CLEOPATRA AND

BRIAN WILLY WONKA WILSON

"YES!" I squeal. "IT'S THE BEST PRIZE EVER!"

And I stuff the foam sausages into my ears and when Mum, Dad and Spike come running in they look a bit like puppets. Their mouths are making funny shapes but I can't hear anything coming out of them! And I get into bed and climb undercover with Wanda beside me, and in total peace and quiet, I doodle...

Dear Frankie,

I promised to tell you my tie breaker if I won! And guess what? I DID! You were right! Here it is in our own secret language...

What a holiday to remember!
I think I'm ready to go back to school!
I'll see you on Monday,
Lots of love and hieroglyphic kisses,
Minnie xxx

# Also available:

I cannot believe it! Mr Impey, our new teacher, has set us homework that is probably my best homework ever! It's a top-secret message that you have to unscramble … and being a secret undercover puzzler, I can't wait to start puzzling it. But there's one very BIG problem that stands in my way, and it comes in the shape of one very small person … my cling-on cousin Dot!

Get **puzzling** with the fabaroony **Minnie Piper**, as she tackles top-secret messages, and some fabulously *fishy* goings on…

My head is fizzing with puzzles and secrets!
Not only am I planning four secret clues to my best-ever birthday party, but a heart-shaped riddle addressed to me has just arrived in this morning's post. It is spottily peculiar and dotted with ladybirds and I haven't a clue who it is from. I'm desperate to show Frankie and start puzzling it out, but Frankie won't stop TALKING!

**Minnie Piper**

**is back!**

**Join her as she puzzles some spottily Secret clues and goes hot on the *trail of* birthday treasure...!**

If you would like to find out more
about **Minnie** and Caroline
why not visit them at

www.fabaroony.co.uk

It's full of fabaroony goings on,

**mind-boggling** puzzles

and *finger-licking,*
*yummy recipes...*

And you can send Caroline your
fabiozo Minnie letters, puzzles and pictures!

See you there Undercover Puzzlers!

!